Life is not always as it appears, and Jordan Maxwell discovers that the truth doesn't always matter. When a beloved rock 'n' roll legend is found dead in his apartment, she is charged with his murder. With her fingerprints lifted from the knife embedded in his chest, her lipstick discovered on his lips, and her clothes covered in his blood, the district attorney figures it's a case of a lovers' spat gone deadly. To him, a guilty verdict is a slam dunk. To make matters worse, when the court of public opinion weighs in, Jordan finds herself catapulted from relative obscurity to the most hated woman in America.

Having once loved Jordan enough to ask her to marry him, Reed Carrington still cares enough about her to want to keep her from going to prison, and he knows he's her best chance.

When he offers to represent her, Jordan knows it's an offer she can't refuse despite the five years of estrangement between them. He's the most sought-after criminal defense attorney in New York, and his reputation is well-earned.

Reed and Jordan both agree that it is crucial to Jordan's defense that they find the murderer. They didn't count on dealing with powerful, lingering feelings while navigating the threat to Jordan's safety and sifting through the increasing pool of suspects. Both tasks feel more daunting than ever when they discover the murderer isn't finished.

Fingerprints, Lipstick and Blood
Copyright © 2022 Josephine Valent
ISBN: 978-1-4874-3550-9
Cover art by Martine Jardin

Published by eXtasy Books Inc

Look for us online at:
www.eXtasybooks.com

Fingerprints, Lipstick and Blood

By

Josephine Valent

DEDICATION

To Steven Tyler. A major talent. I'm a huge fan. Sorry I had to kill your fictional likeness. By the way, I loved your book.

Chapter One

Jordan Maxwell paced the cold, concrete floor, her arms pressed across her chest, her fingers clenched around tensed biceps. The adrenalin blasting through her clashed with the fatigue that threatened to strangle her, marking the beginnings of what she was sure was going to be one heck of a headache. But that was the least of her problems.

She tried to shake the gruesome vision from her mind so she could concentrate on making some sense of the nightmare she found herself in, but it was as embedded in her head as the knife had been in Steve Tanner's chest. He may have lived the life of an idol and might have lived life recklessly by most standards, but he didn't deserve to die. And certainly not so brutally.

The thought that she had been in his home when he was murdered shook her to the core. That she had watched him take his last breath numbed her to the bone.

She dragged her fingers through her hair. Things like this don't happen to girls like me, she thought. She was raised in a quiet, upscale neighborhood, attended a top university, and worked hard at a career as a writer. She managed to get published and have a loyal enough following to live a decent life. She led a quiet existence. She didn't live life in the fast lane.

The explosion of iron crashing against iron thundered in the silence and had her heart slamming against her ribs. She listened as heavy footsteps followed. They were soon muffled by growls and grumbles, then a general stirring of life.

"Jordan Maxwell." A tall, hulking woman in a blue uniform stopped and glared at her from the other side of the bars. She unlocked a tiny opening between the bars and pulled a set of handcuffs from her belt. "Turn around," she barked.

"Where am I going?" She backed up to the bars and offered her wrists to the guard. Home, she prayed. Maybe the police had discovered that they had made a mistake. Maybe they were releasing her. Maybe it was all a nightmare, and when she walked out of the cell, she'd wake up in her apartment.

"Your lawyer's here," the guard answered, and she felt the cold steel cuffs clamp around her wrists.

"My lawyer?" She'd been stripped of everything, including her watch. As best as she could judge, she'd been in jail for only a couple of hours. She hadn't even called anyone. Her throat went dry at the thought that it might be the murderer. Maybe he thought she'd seen him. Maybe he'd come to silence her. She tried to smother the panic before it had a chance to kindle. Don't be ridiculous, she told herself. No one would walk into a police station and kill someone. Besides, it would do no good to get hysterical. She had to try to keep her wits about her. "I didn't call a lawyer," she said as calmly as she could muster.

"Well, somebody did." The guard slid the bars aside. "Let's go." She grabbed her arm and yanked her from the cell.

The cuffs cutting into her flesh were a painful reminder that it wasn't just a bad dream.

"Do I have to be handcuffed?"

"You were arrested on suspicion of murder. They're required."

The words pulled at the knot in her stomach. It was the second time they had been said to her. It was absurd that anyone, especially the police, would think that she had killed Steve Tanner. That they did just twisted the knot tighter.

She offered no resistance, yet the guard's hand was cinched

like a vice around her arm, as if the handcuffs and two hundred pounds of rock-solid muscle towering over her weren't enough. The guard steered her through a door, and they headed down an empty hallway. "Why'd you kill him? I heard it was in a fit of jealousy."

The guard was baiting her. She knew she wouldn't believe her if she denied killing Steve, but she knew if she didn't deny it, her silence could be a mark of admission. "I didn't kill anyone," she answered and felt the guard's fingers tighten.

The caustic laugh that followed scratched through her like a claw through flesh. "If that's your defense, you'd better get yourself ready for a new home, sweetheart."

They turned at the end of the hallway and took a few more steps before the guard spoke again. "Your lawyer should be in here." She pushed open a heavy door. Planting a foot against it, she shoved her into a small room.

Barely past the threshold, Jordan stopped dead in her tracks, somewhere between relief and shock. She fought hard to keep her jaw hinged. *That* she could control, but the jackhammer pace of her heart was a lost cause.

She'd seen Reed Carrington's picture in newspapers over the years. She'd even seen him on a few television news programs, but she never thought she would see him again in person. Yet he was standing less than ten feet from her, staggeringly handsome with his dark, meticulously-groomed hair and magnificently-toned body expertly fitted in the finest custom-made Italian suit. She'd done her best to avoid events and parties she thought he might attend. She'd had no interest in running into him after they had gone their separate ways. To steer clear of him had been the only way for her heart to survive. It had been the only way for her to move on.

"Good morning, Mr. Carrington," the guard gushed and then sidled toward him. "They didn't tell me you were representing Maxwell." The guard's rigid movements softened into a fluid dance as she continued. "It's nice to see you again."

"You as well, Gloria," Reed replied with a slight nod and the kind of smile that made a woman feel like she was all that mattered.

He still had it, Jordan concluded. He'd managed to turn a Rottweiler into a Golden retriever with nothing more than a flick of his lips and a few words. His charm could render a woman defenseless. She knew from personal experience just how powerful it was, and the flutter in her belly reminded her that she wasn't immune to it.

"Thank you." She watched the guard drag her tongue over her top lip, then, with a batting of lashes, sashay back toward the door. "Just knock on the door when you're finished."

"Gloria, do you think you could remove the handcuffs before you leave?"

"Well, it's—"

All it took was a lift of a brow.

"Sure. I suppose I can make an exception for you." The guard took a step toward her, then slid the handcuffs from her wrists.

"Thank you. I appreciate it," he said, once again tossing her a smile.

The guard pranced from the room with a nod and a seductive pucker of lips in return, leaving them alone.

Jordan drew a breath, steadied her heart, and raised her chin. Despite the grotesque oversized pumpkin-orange jumpsuit and the fact that she was now a resident of the county jail, she still had some measure of pride. "Hello, Reed." She managed a smile but kept the distance between them, the coolness in her own voice surprising her. It had been five years. She was over the hurt. She was over the humiliation. She should be able to greet him more warmly. She dismissed the thought, attributing her reaction to the circumstances. "How did you know I was here?"

"You always did like to get straight to the point," he remarked with a smile. "You're front-page news." He lowered himself to the corner of the table beside him and slid his gaze over her. "You're looking well." She watched him draw a breath and then continue. "Actually, that's an understatement. You look beautiful."

"Thank you." Her voice softened, but she knew she looked anything but beautiful. The comment was nothing more than small talk. With not a wink of sleep in over twenty-four hours and the shock of watching a man die, she was sure she'd never looked worse. "What is the media reporting?" she asked, wondering how much information had been released.

"Steve Tanner's murder. And it's on every television and radio news broadcast. Unfortunately" —he frowned— "you were mentioned as the prime suspect."

She took a step toward him, her eyes riveted on his. "Is that why you're here? Because he was famous? Because he's a rock 'n' roll legend?" It made sense. All of the cases she'd read about him handling involved famous people. Surely he wasn't there to do her any favors. Their relationship hadn't ended on good terms, and they hadn't spoken in five years. Still, the thought that he would exploit her for his benefit cut deep, and the feigned flash of hurt she saw in his eyes from her words did little to convince her that he was there for any other reason.

"No, and I'll ignore the affront. I know none of this can be easy for you. The circumstances . . . me." He folded his hands in his lap. "I don't seek fame. I don't solicit people in high-profile situations. Famous people in need of my services solicit me, and I've happened to have enough famous clients to keep me in the news more than I care to be. I don't need any more attention." He pushed himself off the table and pulled back a chair. "Now," he said, gesturing for her to sit. "If you're finished questioning my motives, maybe we can get on with our meeting."

She looked down at the chair, then back up at him, but her resolve stood firm. "If you don't need any more attention, why are you here?" Perhaps it was as much self-preservation as sleep deprivation that had her so guarded with him, but she couldn't help it. After all, he had broken her heart.

"Because you need me. I've spoken with the district attorney handling this case. According to him, your lipstick was found on Tanner's lips, your fingerprints were on the knife buried in his chest, his blood was on your clothes, and his bloody hand print was around your wrist. The DA thinks this is an open and shut case. A simple case of a lovers' spat gone ugly." He hesitated, then pulled his hand from the chair. "You're most likely going to be charged with the murder of Steve Tanner. I've confirmed that the initial arraignment will be set for this afternoon."

The words slammed into her like a punch to the stomach, cutting off her next breath. She hadn't even been given a chance to explain. A river of numbness swept through her, turning her muscles to putty. She felt sick as her eyes lost focus, and the room started spinning around her. She noticed herself collapsing and fought to find the strength to keep from slipping away.

"Jordan."

She heard his voice through the haze. It sounded distant, yet she felt his arms beneath her, holding onto her. It had been a long time since she'd heard him utter her name and since she'd felt his arms around her. The memories flooded back with a vengeance. Ripples of well-toned muscle, skillful hands, powerful rhythm, and explosive passion. It was impossible not to get lost in it.

"Jordan, can you hear me?" She heard his voice again. He

was asking her something. He was so close. She could taste his breath. She whispered his name.

"I'm here, Jordan. Everything's going to be all right." His voice was clearer this time. She could make out his words. The fog was drifting away, and when she blinked, she found herself staring into the eyes of a man with such pull he could make a woman step out of her clothes with just the curve of his lips.

"No," she managed as she tried to wriggle free. "Put me down. I . . . I just need to sit down."

He lowered her to the chair and let go of her.

She tried to push aside the onslaught of memories as she watched him pour some water into a paper cup from a plastic pitcher on the table.

"Here," he said and handed her the cup. "Drink this."

Her mind was still spinning somewhere between the past and the present, but her pulse was still reacting to the past. She took a sip and hoped it would flush away the memories. She watched him pull the other chair around, position it to face hers, and sit down.

"Are you all right? Was this a reaction to what I said, or do you have a medical condition? Do I need to get you medical attention or medication?"

The concern in his voice was unmistakable, and when she lifted her gaze to his, it was evident in his eyes. Whether it was sincere was another matter, she decided. "I'm fine." She shook her head. "It's just lack of sleep. And I think everything that's happened is catching up to me."

He reached for her hand and held it between his. "I want you to know that I'm here for you. I'm damn good at what I do. I'm your best chance of getting out of this situation, and I will do everything in my power to keep you from going to prison."

"Okay." She nodded and drew her hand from his. She

didn't have much choice. She needed him. She was well aware of his reputation of being the best criminal defense attorney in New York. She was just going to have to deal with the fact that he would be in her life again. "Thank you." She needed to think about her future, not her past. She took a breath and, feeling better, stood up. She rounded the chair, rested her palms on the top of the backrest, and peered down at him. "I'm sure you'll agree that our . . . parting . . . wasn't the most amicable of partings. I'd like to make sure that our past stays in the past."

"Our . . . parting?" He lifted a brow and stood up. He stepped toward her, towering over her five-five by a good eight inches. He leaned down and slid his hands over hers. The chair might have separated their bodies, but only a whisper of air came between their lips. "You left me."

"I didn't have a choice." She tried to pull away, but his hands were like a dead weight over hers.

"You could have married me."

She took a step back and snatched her hands free. His closeness had set off a spark of electricity that shot straight down to her toes. "It was complicated."

"It seemed quite simple to me." He pushed himself back from the chair. "I asked you to marry me, you said yes, then you left me. But" — he took a step back, dragged the chair to the other side of the table, and sat down — "I agree with you. Our past is best left behind us." He motioned for her to sit back down.

"Good." She nodded and lowered herself to the chair. "We'll just keep this strictly professional."

"Strictly professional." He nodded. "Now, about this afternoon."

CHAPTER TWO

As Reed had anticipated, the afternoon proceedings went without a glitch and were over in a matter of minutes. He and the district attorney said a few words, and the judge set the bail amount. The bail was paid, and Jordan was released from jail. Though it all went as expected, he couldn't help but feel relieved. After all, he had once loved her. They'd had a serious history together, and he still cared enough about her that he didn't want to see her sitting in jail. Besides, he had a personal stake in the case. Getting her to fall in love with him again was not going to be easy if she was in jail. Now that she was out, he could proceed with his plan.

He hadn't expected the mob of reporters, cameramen, and Steve Tanner fans that had jammed the courtroom, flooded the courthouse hallways, and packed the front steps of the courthouse. He'd expected the media coverage and a reasonable number of onlookers, but not the horde gathered. As always, however, he had prepared for the worst.

"Why are all these people here?" Jordon asked once they had made it to the limousine.

"Steve Tanner apparently has a lot of fans, and it seems they all want to get a look at you." He glanced through the blackened windows at the crowd still surrounding them. "There are probably two generations of fans out there. What the—" He threw his arm across Jordan as the limousine started to rock, and the mob surrounding them began to chant. They started covering the limousine like a swarm of angry bees.

"What's going on? What are they doing?" She grabbed his arm as she looked out at the bodies crushed against the limousine. "Where did the bodyguards go?"

"They'll be back." He pulled her from the seat in one rapid movement, shoved her toward the front, and shielded her body with his. Nobody was going to get to her without going through him first. He banged on the window separating them from his driver, and it lowered. "Get moving. Get us out of here."

"Sir, I'm trying," the driver replied, his frustration evident as he slammed his hand against the horn and cursed at the crowd.

The limousine bucked and pitched like a wild bronco, and fists pounded down on it like thundering hooves. They were being assaulted from all sides. Reed struggled to brace himself and to hold onto Jordan. She was trembling, and he heard her scream when something hard crashed against the back window, fracturing it into a million pieces. One more blow would have it caving in.

"Hit the damn gas," he yelled. "They'll move."

"Yes, sir." The driver inched the vehicle forward, the entire time blasting the horn. The rocking ceased, but the bombardment continued. Something heavy smashed against the car, and when Reed glanced up, he caught a glimpse of a trash bin bouncing off of the car's trunk, garbage spewing everywhere. A dark SUV nudged the crowd behind them aside and pulled up behind them. He recognized the bodyguards inside. He watched as they created a diversion, and the mob surrounding them began to disburse.

The limousine picked up speed as the driver took advantage of the people stepping aside and a gap in traffic. The barrage diminished to a pelting, and after they'd run two red lights, the attack ended. They were a safe distance away. When he felt Jordan release the two handfuls of silk from the sleeves of his suit, he slid onto the seat next to her and relaxed his grip. "Are you all right?" He could feel her still trembling.

"Yes," she managed.

"John, are you all right?" he called to the driver.

"I'm fine, sir. Is everything all right back there?"

"Yes. Just get us to the office."

"Yes, sir." The window between them slid up.

"Those people hate me."

He could hear the fear in Jordan's voice.

"They think I killed Steve."

"Right now, what happened is raw, and you're the focus of attention. That will change with the next headline, and things will calm down eventually." In the meantime, it was game on. She had walked away from him five years ago. It was time to remind her of what she had walked away from. He'd make sure she was stuck with him until he cleared her. By then, if things went according to his plan, she'd be in love with him again. And this time, he was going to be the one to walk away. He was going to have to be careful, though. Loving her had been easy. His love for her had once saturated every fiber of his being. He would have to make sure to keep his heart at a safe distance this time.

"Why are we going to your office?" When she tried to stifle a yawn, he could see that the past twelve hours had worn on her. Regardless, she's holding up well, he thought as he studied her. She'd barely been out of college when she'd left him. Her pretty, girlish looks had been replaced by a refined exquisiteness. Her hair was shorter, just touching her shoulders, which enhanced the sleek line of her jaw and the defined bones in her cheeks. Her porcelain skin was still flawless, and her full, lush lips were just as enticing.

"I don't think you should go home for a few days." The wheels were already in motion. She'd be with him tonight.

"I have to go home." Though she tried to protest, the words

tumbled from her lips with little conviction, and he knew she wouldn't put up much resistance.

"I don't think you have a choice. That crowd is probably heading to your home, but don't worry. I'll make sure you're safe and comfortable where you'll be staying." He glanced out of the window as the limousine turned down an alley. They were only about two blocks from his office. They were going to enter the building from the rear. The building's security staff had strict instructions to clear the lobby and not let anyone inside the building when they arrived. The service elevator would be waiting for them to take them directly to the penthouse floor of the firm's offices.

"Where will that be?"

"At my home in Water Mill." He waited for the objection. He anticipated it, but she was silent for a long moment.

"I didn't know you had a home in Water Mill. I'd prefer not to intrude on your personal life."

"Don't worry, you won't be. I don't have much of one at the moment." He watched the back door of the building swing open, and a security guard stepped out. The limousine came to a halt, and the door locks popped up. He leaned down and grabbed his briefcase from the floor where it had come to rest after the ruckus.

The guard pulled open the limousine door and nodded to the SUV behind them. "It's all clear, Mr. Carrington," he announced.

"Let's go." Reed took Jordan's hand and led her from the vehicle. Once outside, he wrapped a protective arm around her waist. It was enough to make his gut react, just as it had that morning when he'd held her in his arms. The feel of her curves under the fabric, the flavor of her scent in his lungs, and the sound of his name from her lips had ignited a spark on a long-extinguished flame. He'd anticipated physical reactions, of course, but not as sharp. Their passion had run deep, but five years had passed between them.

They followed the guard inside. He escorted them into the elevator, punched the button to the top floor, and then hopped out. He stood in place while the doors slid shut.

As the elevator began its ascent, Reed released his arm from around her waist and put a little needed distance between them, wondering if he had underestimated the power of her draw. He dismissed the thought and focused on the priority at hand. "We should discuss what happened with you and Tanner while it's still fresh in your mind, and so I can put some things in motion here before we leave for Water Mill." He could see the weariness in her eyes and planned to keep his questions brief. He'd get just enough information to give his investigator something to start working on.

"I'm going to need to get some clothes and a toothbrush."

"That's been taken care of." He glanced up at the flashing numbers for each floor they passed and then looked down at her. Hair like silk, eyes like emeralds, and lips as soft as rose petals. He remembered the feel of those lips on his as vividly as he remembered the smoothness of her flesh against his. It had been a mistake to let her leave, and he wondered how he could have ever let her go. Pride, he recalled. Damn pride. She'd had hers. He'd had his.

She nodded, then glanced down at her new *Chanel* suit and pumps. "Thank you for having the outfit delivered for the hearing."

"You're welcome. I prefer you in green rather than orange," he said with a grin. The elevator slid to a stop at the penthouse suite, and when the doors parted, he ushered her into the middle of a long hallway. It was a quiet area with only the humming of office machines emanating from the offices along the corridor. "My office is this way," he said, guiding her down the hallway. "Are you hungry? Would you like me to send out for some supper?"

"No, but some coffee would be nice."

"No problem. This way." They rounded a corner and entered an open area in the center of the suite. Beams of sunlight fell upon them, glistening through massive skylights that circled the edge of the ceiling. Crystals twinkled from enormous chandeliers that adorned the center of the ceiling. Below it all was a circular area surrounded by a rich, marble counter that separated the workers inside from the offices hidden behind tall, richly-carved doors that lined the outer area of the suite. Opulence, he thought as he imagined his father and his stuffy old partners designing the suite just to stroke their egos and impress their wealthy clients.

He recalled how the partners had balked at the idea of him joining the firm and practicing criminal law. They didn't want sleazy criminals associated with their good name, they'd said, until one of the firm's well-respected, high-profile clients was charged with shooting his wife when she'd threatened to divorce him and take half his fortune. He got the client acquitted, and the client walked away a free man. After that, he had doubled the firm's profits and its client list, and the partners no longer discriminated when it came to his clients.

Workers not strapped to earphones or otherwise occupied looked up and acknowledged them with either a nod or a smile when they passed. Some of the stares lingered longer than others, but each had taken the full measure of Jordan. He knew they were aware of who she was and why she was there, and he knew that out of loyalty to him, what happened within the firm's walls would stay there.

Just beyond the circular area, they approached his office. He pushed open the door and escorted Jordan into the small reception area that also served as his secretary's office.

"Good afternoon, Mr. Carrington." As was routine, his secretary took his briefcase in one hand and extended her arm for his suit coat which he slid off and folded over her arm. She offered a warm smile to Jordan before she lowered the brief-case to the floor and proceeded to a nearby closet. "Is there anything I can get you, Mr. Carrington?" she asked as she hung up his coat.

"Yes, Rose. Could you please order Ms. Maxwell and me some coffee?"

"Already done, sir. Will there be anything else?"

"No, and thank you." He pushed through another door and led Jordan into his office. He knew she would find it impressive with its floor-to-ceiling windows, which offered a magnificent view of the city, and the well-appointed, separate sitting area offered a luxurious place to enjoy it. And right now, she was the only one he cared to impress. "Please, make yourself comfortable," he said, gesturing toward the sitting area.

"Thank you." He watched as she made her way toward a chair. A young assistant entered the office, then scurried passed her with a tray. On it were two *Fabergé* cups and saucers, a matching creamer, sugar bowl and coffee pot, and an assortment of baked goods. Jordan smiled at the girl while she placed the tray on the table and then poured the coffee. She sat down as the girl retreated from the office.

He took the chair across from her. "A splash of cream, no sugar," he said before she had even lifted a hand to the tray.

"Is that a guess?" she asked, reaching for the creamer.

"Some things you don't forget," he answered with a shrug. There wasn't much he'd forgotten about her, and he had no doubt that would work in his favor.

"That hardly seems worth remembering."

"I suppose that depends on who's doing the remembering. Anyway" — he leaned down and snatched a pad of paper and a pen from somewhere under the table — "why don't you tell me what happened." He slid back in the chair, crossed one leg over the other, and lifted his gaze to her. "Start from when you last saw Tanner alive."

She took a sip of coffee, then held the cup between her hands. "It was at his apartment. I was with him when he died."

"He wasn't dead when you found him?"

"No. I was upstairs in one of the bedrooms. We'd been at a nightclub together, and I'd left before him, about two-thirty. I was still awake when he got back, about an hour after I did. I heard a loud voice, or voices, downstairs. I couldn't tell if it was one voice or two. It . . . or they . . . were muffled."

"Was there anyone else in the apartment when you got there?"

"No. No one else was staying there, if that's what you mean." She paused for a moment and then took another sip. "I suppose there could have been someone there without my knowing it. You know, hiding. It was Steve's apartment. I don't know who else had access to it."

"What did you do when you heard the voices?" He jotted down a few notes as she continued.

"I was typing. I stopped to listen and closed my laptop. I was trying to figure out how many voices there were and if they were boisterous or angry."

"Did you make that determination?" He finished his notes and looked back up.

"No. The voices stopped, and I heard a crash, then a thud. Steve had been drinking, so the first thing that had come to my mind was that he'd fallen and broken a lamp or a vase or something on his way down. I got up from the desk and rushed downstairs." He could see her body tense. He watched as she set the cup down and crossed her arms over her chest. "When I got downstairs, I found him lying on the floor."

"And he was still alive?"

"Yes. At that point, I didn't know he'd been stabbed." He

heard the stress in her voice increase as she continued. "He was lying on his side, and his back was toward me. I ran over to him, and I knelt down beside him. Then . . . then I rolled him over." He watched as her body shuddered, her hands tightened around her arms, and the color drained from her face. "That's when I saw the . . . the knife in his chest."

"I know this is difficult." She was still shaken, and he didn't want to push her too far. "Do you want to take a break?"

"No. I'd like to get this over with," she insisted. "As you said, I need to tell you what happened while it's still fresh in my mind."

"Okay. I have just a few more questions. Did he say anything to you when you were kneeling beside him?"

"No." She shook her head and drew a shaky breath. "He put his fingers around my wrist and lifted my hand to the knife. He closed his fingers over mine, around the handle of the knife. I think he wanted me to pull the knife out. He tried to say something, but no words came out."

"Then what happened?"

"His hand slid off of mine, and he went limp. I thought . . . or I was hoping that he had passed out. I tried to revive him."

"You rendered CPR?"

"Yes. Just the breaths. I couldn't . . . the knife . . . I couldn't do the chest compressions."

He tossed the pen and pad onto the table, then stood up. He slid his hands into his trouser pockets and paced the office as he churned over what she'd told him. It explained her lipstick on Tanner's lips, his bloody hand print on her wrist, his blood on her clothes, and her fingerprints on the knife. After a moment, he stopped and turned to her. "Which hand of yours did he place on the knife?"

"My right. Why?"

"Are you sure?"

"Yes."

"You're left-handed." This is good, he thought. "The DA thinks there was a struggle between you and Tanner. His theory is that Tanner grabbed your wrist to wrestle the knife away from you. It wouldn't make sense for you to attack him with the knife in your right hand if you're left-handed."

"That's true. I suppose it wouldn't."

"Jordan, what—" He stopped, a commotion just outside the door interrupting him. He turned toward the noise, and a man burst into his office. Rose was behind him with a fist full of his shirt in her hand.

"Where is Jordan Maxwell?" the man demanded.

It took only a split-second for him to get to the man and pin him against the wall. He shoved his forearm against the back of his neck. "Move one muscle, and I'll snap your neck," he growled. He'd had enough of angry Steve Tanner fans for one day, and he wasn't going to let this one get anywhere near Jordan.

"I tried to stop him, Mr. Carrington," Rose said. "I'll call security," she added as she rushed out the door.

"Charles?" Jordan inquired from behind him. "Charles, what are you doing here?"

"Looking for you," the man managed.

"You know him?" he asked. He relaxed his arm but kept the man pinned.

"Yes. It's okay. You can let him go."

He released his grip, but not without warning, "You've got two minutes before I have you thrown out of here." He raked his gaze over the man. Snobby, bookish type, he concluded. Wire frames, plaid jacket. Bad taste. Except for his taste for Jordan. Instantly, he disliked him.

The man reached for Jordan's hand with hardly a glance at him. "Are you all right? I saw the news. I saw the crowd outside of the courthouse trying to get to you. How can they possibly charge you with murder?" His voice sputtered with nervous energy.

"I—"

He cut her off before she could answer and turned to Reed. "I've heard of you. You're supposed to be a good lawyer. I hope you're doing everything you can for Jordan."

"He is, Charles," she assured him. "You don't need to worry about me."

"I went by your apartment. The whole block is teeming with reporters and camera crews. You can't go home. You can come with me," he offered. "I have a cabin in Pennsylvania. It's—"

"All right. That's enough," Reed cut in. As far as he was concerned, she wasn't going anywhere with this poindexter. As Rose returned with two security guards, he gestured to the guards. "Escort this gentleman downstairs, please."

"Reed, just a minute." Jordan tossed him a pleading look, then turned back to the man. "Thank you for your offer. That's very kind of you, Charles," she said as she slid her hand from his. "I have a place to stay, and I'll be there for only a few days before returning to my apartment. I'll call you when I get home."

"Where will you be staying? How will I get in touch with you?"

"That's private," Reed answered for her. "I'm sure you understand, Charles." He gave a quick nod to the guards.

"Right. Of course." He called over his shoulder as the guards ushered him through the door, "Call me the minute you get home."

"I didn't realize you had such varied taste in men these days," Reed remarked as he closed the door behind them. The truth was, he'd known about Tanner. Aside from the fact that he'd kept tabs on Jordan, according to his source, photos of her and Tanner had been in all the society pages and in the tabloids. The poindexter, however, was a surprise. And not a pleasant one. "A rock star and a, what, a bookkeeper?"

"First of all, not that it's any of your business what my taste in men is, Charles is a friend, and I wasn't dating Steve."

"Really." He strode toward his desk as he continued. "What do you call sleeping with someone? And, by the way, it is my business. Now, everything about you is my business."

"I'll let that go because, frankly, I'm too tired to argue with you. The truth is, I wasn't sleeping with Steve. I was working with him."

He looked up from the papers he had started shuffling through. "On what?"

"On his biography." She walked over and faced him from across his desk. "He hired me to write his biography."

He cocked a skeptical brow. "And I suppose your partying and sleeping with him all over Manhattan and the Caribbean was just research?"

"Yes, as a matter of fact. No." She set her hands down on the edge of the desk. "I never drank anything stronger than club soda when I was out with him, and we never slept together. He was always a perfect gentleman with me. Our professional relationship grew into a mutual fondness . . . mutual, personal respect for each other. There was never a physical attraction between us. What we had was purely platonic."

"That's not how it was reported."

"He let everyone assume what they wanted to about me . . . about . . . us. He didn't want anyone to know he'd hired me to write his biography."

"You're serious." He'd known her well enough to know she was telling the truth. "Well, that pokes another big hole in the DA's lovers' spat theory. Who knew what your involvement with Tanner was actually about? Your agent, I assume."

"Nobody." She dropped to one of the client chairs facing

his desk. "As I said, he didn't want anyone to know."

"If he hired you, you have a contract, right?"

She shook her head. "He said he never signs anything until his agent passes it by his attorneys, and he didn't want to risk, in his words, anyone in their offices looking to make a fast buck finding out and spilling it to the tabloids."

"Mr. Carrington." Rose's voice spilled over the intercom. "The helicopter is waiting."

"Thank you. Let the pilot know we're on our way up." He looked across the desk. "We'll continue this conversation when we get to Water Mill." He tossed a file into his briefcase and snapped it shut. "Shall we?"

CHAPTER THREE

Jordan's eyes fluttered open, and she felt a light breeze caress her cheek. Rays of soft sunlight sneaking through the swaying drapes bathed her in warmth. It took a moment before she realized that she was awake and another before she remembered where she was.

With a moan, she rolled over and wished that she could stay in bed until the nightmare with Steve Tanner was over. It was enough to be grieving the loss of such a wonderful man, but the circumstances of his death made it more agonizing. She glanced at a nearby clock and realized that she'd slept for nearly ten hours. By the time they'd arrived in Water Mill the night before, she had acquired a monster of a headache. It had felt as if someone had taken a sledgehammer to her skull, and she'd been relieved that Reed didn't press her to finish their discussion about what had happened. Instead, he'd taken her straight upstairs and said they'd talk more in the morning after she was rested.

He's probably waiting for me, she thought. Despite the nearly half-day of sleep, she still felt drained. It would take a few nights of good, deep sleep to get herself adjusted to keeping regular hours again after the schedule she had kept with Steve.

She slid her legs over the side of the bed and sat up. She let her gaze travel over the enormous bedroom. The entire suite was decorated in a beautiful Tuscan flavor with its exquisite wall tapestries and intricate scrolled iron panels. It reminded her of a lovely villa on Lake Como she'd once stayed in on a trip to Italy with her parents.

She pushed herself up from the bed and decided on a shower before going downstairs.

Within half an hour, she was feeling better, and having put on a blouse and pair of jeans from the shopping bags of clothes purchased for her, she headed downstairs.

The house was quiet, and she took her time admiring it as she made her way down the sweeping staircase. From the night before, she remembered the deep cherry wood floor that spanned the foyer. It was even more vibrant with the sunlight streaming across it. The entire house could have been transplanted there from Tuscany, from what she saw. It's warm, charming, and a pleasant diversion from the city, she thought as she felt her spirits lift.

She followed the soft music that could be heard when she approached the foot of the stairs. As she got closer, she could make out a woman's voice humming along. She could have sworn Reed had told her the day before that he wasn't married. Maybe she'd misunderstood, or perhaps they hadn't discussed the topic at all. After all, it had been a stressful and exhausting day, and his personal life hadn't been the focus of it.

She stopped just outside of a closed door to listen to the voice and caught herself frowning at the thought that the woman could be Reed's wife or a girlfriend or a fiancée. When she felt a little prick to her heart, she shifted uncomfortably. *I cannot possibly have any lingering feelings for him,* she assured herself, *not after five years. It must be something else, most likely fatigue.* She waved it off, pushed open the door, and stepped into the kitchen.

The woman looked up when she entered. A smile beamed across the woman's face, and she let the spoon she was stirring something with drop to the side of the bowl. "I wondered when you'd be joining the living," she said in a thick, Irish accent as she wiped her hands on the well-worn apron wrapped around her plump, round body. She spread her arms and took a few strides over to Jordan.

"Mrs. Doyle, how nice it is to see you," Jordan said, surprised. She stepped into Mrs. Doyle's chubby arms and returned the hearty embrace.

"Let me look at you now," Mrs. Doyle said, taking a step back and taking an extended survey of Jordan. "Your hair's shorter, but you look just as pretty as you did the last time I saw you."

"Thank you, and you're looking well." The rosy-red cheeks were just a little fuller, and the tightly spun bun was now just a little more white than blonde, but the light blue eyes were just as full of spirit as she remembered.

"A bottle or two of *Guinness* at the end of the day," she said with a wink. "That's what keeps the aches and pains away." She led her to a large, rustic table and pulled out a chair. "Now, sit right down here. Let me make you some breakfast. You must be famished. Reed told me you didn't eat dinner last night."

"Please, don't go to any trouble," she replied, wondering what else he'd told her. "It looks like you're in the middle of making something."

"Oh, I'm always in the middle of making something. The kitchen is my favorite room in the house, you know." She set the bowl with the spoon aside and rummaged through a nearby cupboard. "What would you like?" She continued before Jordan had a chance to answer. "How 'bout I cook you up some eggs and sausage with some potatoes and black pudding? Oh, and I have some fresh brown bread I made just yesterday."

Jordan didn't have much appetite, her stomach still not quite settled from the day before. She would've been happy with just toast and a cup of coffee, but she didn't want to offend Mrs. Doyle. She remembered that Mrs. Doyle liked to fuss over people and that she'd get a little ruffled if they didn't let her. "I'm not that hungry, but an egg and some toast would be nice."

"Certainly, and a cup of coffee, too, I assume?" She flipped the switch to brew on the coffeemaker without waiting for her answer. "Seems nobody drinks tea anymore."

"May I help with anything?"

"Heavens, no," she answered with a chuckle. "I don't need any help to prepare a meal for just one person."

"Do you still work for Reed's parents?" The last time she'd seen Mrs. Doyle, she was employed as a housekeeper in his parents' household. She remembered meeting her when she and Reed had started dating during her first year of college. He had already started law school by then. They had continued dating for three and a half more years until she'd graduated from college and Reed was well into his first job as a lawyer. That was when he had proposed to her. She remembered how thrilled Mrs. Doyle had been about their engagement.

"No. And thank goodness, I might add."

She watched Mrs. Doyle pull a couple of eggs from the refrigerator as she continued.

"I never liked serving the missus. She was too uppity for my tastes. I'm sure you know what I mean." She glanced over her shoulder and tossed her a wink. "Anyway, I always felt like my job was done there once Reed had grown up and moved on. One day, I asked him if he could ask the young attorneys at his fancy law firm if any of them needed a nanny. You know, I was his nanny until he outgrew me. Anyway, wouldn't you know it, bless his heart, he said he couldn't live without me and offered me a job taking care of his house here. And here, I have my own little cottage. Back there." She nodded toward the door. "At the edge of the property."

She wondered what her life would be like had Reed felt the same way about her five years ago, then brushed the thought aside. No thinking about the past, she reminded herself. "Sounds like you raised a good man. And speaking about Reed, do you know where he is?"

"He should be back any minute. I sent him to the market. Told him he could either make you breakfast when you woke up or go to the market. I couldn't do both. He called me yesterday to tell me you were coming. That only gave me enough time to make it to the butcher's, with everything else I had to do around here."

Jordan got up when she saw that the coffee had finished dripping into the carafe but was shooed back to the table with a wave of Mrs. Doyle's dish towel.

"Just sit right back down. Reed's gone most of the time, so let me do my job when he is here. Besides, after yesterday, it seems you could use a little spoiling."

"I take it Reed told you the reason I'm here?"

"He didn't have to." She set a cup and saucer on the table in front of her. "I saw it on the news. Seems you got yourself into a little scrape."

"Yes, it does seem that way," she agreed. She stirred a drop of cream into the coffee and then lifted the cup to her lips and took a sip. The coffee was dark and robust.

"Well, you needn't worry," she assured her as she waddled back toward the stove. "You have the best lawyer in the world on your side. I'm sure Reed will prove you're innocent."

"I hope so. Spending the rest of my life in prison doesn't sound appealing."

"I imagine not, but don't you think about that." She placed a dish of eggs with a couple of slices of brown bread on the table. "Now, tell me what you've been doing with yourself all these years," she said as she headed back to the bowl she had set aside. "Did you ever go and get yourself married after you left Reed standing at the altar?"

She had to swallow hard to prevent choking on the bite she had just taken. "No," she replied after she was confident the egg had passed down her throat. "And I didn't leave Reed. And certainly not at any altar. We were barely engaged."

"That's not how he saw it," Mrs. Doyle said, shaking her head. "The poor boy—" She stopped at the sound of bags being juggled outside and then hurried to the door. "Let me help you with that." She pushed against the screen door and flung it open. "You've got your arms full."

She wondered for a second what Mrs. Doyle was about to say but lost the thought when Reed came through the door, his arms loaded with bags. Despite her best effort, she couldn't convince herself that it was something other than the sight of him that had her pulse quicken.

"That was quite a list you gave me. One would think you were cooking for an army," he remarked as he set the bags on the counter. The moment his eyes met hers, he smiled. "Well, look who's awake. As out of it as you were last night, I didn't think I'd see you until well after noon." She didn't miss it when he stuffed a newspaper behind the bags. She assumed she was still headline news and that it wasn't flattering if he didn't want her to see it.

"Really?" She returned the smile and arched a brow. "Is that why you opted to go grocery shopping rather than cook me breakfast?"

"It was out of an abundance of caution that I opted to go to the market rather than risk having to cook." He strode over to the table, dragged out a chair, and sat down. "And you should be grateful for that."

"Can I get you a cup of coffee, dearie?" Mrs. Doyle called from across the kitchen, where Jordan noticed she was already emptying the bags.

"No, I'll get it," he called back.

"You just stay where you are and let me do my job," she scolded him as she abandoned the groceries and pulled a cup and saucer from the cupboard.

"I think if I let her, she'd be stuffing napkins down my collar and wiping crumbs off my face," he teased.

"I'd hope I taught you to do that on your own by now," she said, setting the cup and saucer on the table.

Jordan was sure she had. She recalled Reed once telling her that Mrs. Doyle had pretty much raised him and that he'd hardly even seen his mother growing up. She remembered thinking how lucky she'd been to have parents who had wanted to spend as much time with her as they could. Her parents had taken her everywhere with them. She'd rarely been left with the staff, let alone a full-time nanny.

"Oh, my. I completely forgot I started doing laundry this morning," Mrs. Doyle remarked with a head shake. "I've got linens in the dryer that need to be folded. Give me a shout if you need anything." She turned and scurried out of the kitchen.

Jordan glanced down at her plate, deciding if she had the appetite and the room to eat anything more.

"You better eat all your eggs before she gets back," Reed joked. "You might get a talking to if she thinks you haven't eaten enough."

"I don't doubt that," she replied with a smile and lifted her gaze to Reed. "That was a nice thing you did for her, hiring her, giving her a place of her own to live."

"I owe her," he replied, snatching a piece of bread from her plate. "She was more of a mother to me than my own mother was."

"That may be true, but not everyone would do what you've done."

"Not everyone had Mrs. Doyle looking after them, either." He took a drink of coffee, then got up and strolled over to where he had set down the grocery bags. "She's a little forget-ful." He took a gallon container of milk and a carton of eggs from one of the bags and put them in the refrigerator. "But she's a hell of a cook."

"She was always very nice to me." Deciding she'd better save room for lunch if it was going to be as big a meal as breakfast, she got up and carried her plate to the sink.

"That's because she liked you."

She watched him toss a bag of potatoes in the pantry, then rest against the counter and settle his gaze on her while fold-ing an empty bag.

She turned and placed her dish in the sink. She knew he was studying her. She could feel the intensity of his gaze as she washed her plate and then set it in the drying rack. She reached over for the pan that Mrs. Doyle had used for cooking the eggs, and a wisp of heat drifted through her. Old reactions die hard, she told herself. Once, he had been able to make her blood simmer without as much as a touch. She vowed that she wouldn't give him that power again and drew a deep breath to cool the heat.

She grabbed the dish detergent from the edge of the sink and squeezed a drop into the pan. She didn't need to look over her shoulder to know he was closing the distance be-tween them. She sensed it. She could feel his pull. It was like a rip tide.

When she felt his hands on her shoulders, she braced her-self for the assault, and when he slid his hands down her arms, she closed her eyes as the sparks ignited. His fingers grazed her wrists and then lifted the pan from her grasp just as it was about to slip from her hand. He set the pan down. He was so close she could feel his breath on her neck. "Let Mrs. Doyle finish cleaning up. Come with me."

His touch had set off a firestorm inside her, and she was sure he'd noticed. "Where?" She had to fight hard to regain her composure and keep her voice from betraying her.

He took a step back. "Outside." Then, he reached for a dish towel and tossed it to her. "Let's take a walk down to the water. You can finish telling me about Tanner."

She nodded, then cursed herself for almost turning to mush in his arms. If she couldn't control old reactions, she would have to keep a safe distance between them until she could. *He means nothing to me,* she reminded herself. She dried her hands and followed him outside. "You have a lovely home," she said, searching for something innocuous to discuss as they started across the lawn. She needed a distraction, and at the moment, his home was as good a topic as any.

"Thanks. I bought it for tax purposes, originally. Then, when Mrs. Doyle asked me to find her another job, I realized that it could also serve another purpose. It makes her feel useful. Managing this place keeps her busy. And having the small house on the rear of the property for her was a nice little bonus. It gave her a place she could call home."

"Did you purchase it as is, or did you have it decorated?"

"That's all my work," he answered. "Working on this house gave me something to do when I came here. I wasn't intending to spend much time here when I bought the place, but after I moved Mrs. Doyle here, I found myself coming here more often, you know, to check on her, make sure she wasn't lonely, that sort of thing."

"How long ago did you buy it?"

He shrugged. "I don't know, a few years ago."

They strolled in silence for a short distance until they reached the bay. The light breeze skimming off the water offered just the proper relief from the scorching sun.

"Do you have any idea who might have killed Tanner?"

"No. I don't." She reached down and slid off her shoes. "He didn't seem like the type of person who made enemies."

"Who did he talk about with you?" He stopped beside her,

pulled off his own shoes, then took hers and tossed both pairs onto the beach. "If you were writing his biography and doing it confidentially, it seems like he would be willing to talk pretty freely with you."

"One would think that, but he didn't." She took a few steps closer to the water's edge. The waves were a gentle lap and rolled over her feet, reaching her ankles. "He wanted me to meet his children and the friends he was close with first."

She had met all of his children, and the thought that they might think she had killed Steve, that she could hurt him, and them, had gnawed at her from the moment she'd been arrested. She didn't call them because she was unsure if calling them would ease their pain or worsen it, and she didn't want to risk the latter.

"His children? How many does he have?"

"Four total." While he paused and glanced behind them, she bent down and scooped up a shell. "He had two daughters with a woman named Janine Jones. They're in their late thirties. He had a boy several years later with Claire Douglas, the actress. And he said he fathered a child after that marriage broke up that he'd recently found out about."

"That's interesting. Did he mention a name?"

"He wouldn't say." She dropped the shell, and they continued strolling along the water's edge. "He wouldn't say who the mother was, either. He said he would tell me in due time."

"What do you think he meant by that?"

"I don't know." She shrugged. "I asked him when he thought that would be. I assumed he was still trying to figure out if he could trust me. Although I felt after spending almost twenty-four hours a day with him for five weeks, doing everything he'd asked of me, and no one having found out why I was tagging along with him, that I had earned his trust."

"What did he say?"

"Again, in due time." She released a long sigh. "It looks like Steve Tanner's secrets died with him."

"Not necessarily. There are often at least two parties to a secret."

"Are you thinking someone killed Steve because of something he knew about someone? To silence him?"

"It's possible." He stopped, bent down, and picked up a rock. He turned it over and then tossed it into his other hand.

She stopped beside him and watched while he threw the stone back into the water. "No one would have killed him to stop him from disclosing some sort of a secret. No one knew I was writing his biography," she reminded him. "There was no reason for anyone to think their secret was in jeopardy of being told."

"That you're aware of," he corrected her. "Maybe someone found out."

"That's not possible. Steve and I were the only ones who knew, and Steve was adamant that no one else knew what we were doing. He wouldn't have told anyone, and I didn't."

"I'm just exploring a theory." He glanced back down the beach, then met her gaze.

"I think you're wasting your time with that one."

"All right. Let's try another theory." He took a step back. "Tell me who you've slept with in the last year."

"What?" She jumped at the tangle of seaweed that had come in with a wave and looped around her ankle. She nearly tumbled onto the sand, trying to shake it loose, and felt his arm slide beneath her. He steadied her and drew her into him. She knew it would be a lost cause to resist when he tightened his grip. He could out-muscle her, but she sure as hell wouldn't let her body react as it had in the kitchen. He had caught her off guard in the kitchen. She was prepared now. Whatever game he was playing, she would beat him at it. "All right, let's see." She crumpled her lips. "There was

Thomas . . . Richard . . . Harold . . ."

"Tom, Dick, and Harry. That's cute. Let's see if we can get a rise out of that guy watching us back there," he said with a slight tilt of his head. "Don't look," he added as she was about to turn her head. Before she could say a word, his lips had covered hers, and she had no choice but to kiss him back. The heat swept through her with a fury, and memories flashed through her mind with lightning speed. She felt like she was being pulled back to the past.

She was losing whatever willpower she might have thought she had. If he didn't release her, he'd know the kiss was becoming as much hers as it was his, and that was something she wouldn't risk. If it was passion he wanted, it was passion he would get. She traded the lust swirling through her for anger and pushed him back. "What the hell do you think you're doing?"

"Calm down," he said with a smirk, still holding on to her. "As I said, I'm just testing a theory."

"And what theory is that? How big an ass you can be?"

"My, you do have a temper." He released her and then looked back down the beach. "He turned around. Seems to be in a hurry, too. If he were the paparazzi, he wouldn't be leaving. He'd be all over us trying to get a picture." He looked down at her. "Are you going to give me that list or not?"

"No." She knew she wasn't going to win the argument that it was none of his business, but she wouldn't tell him about the men she had dated since they had split. His ego was big enough. She wouldn't inflate it any more than it already was by telling him she hadn't managed to have a serious relationship since theirs. "You'll just have to believe that it wasn't anyone I dated that killed Steve."

"Maybe," he said and turned back toward the figure. "Maybe not."

Chapter Four

R eed smiled to himself. It had been over a month since he'd brought Jordan to Water Mill, and he was sure that she still had lingering feelings for him. She was keeping her guard up, though. Every time he touched her, he could feel the conflict inside her. She wanted to give in, but she'd find the resolve to resist. He was wearing her down, but it was killing him. He wanted her so badly it was nearly driving him insane.

He picked up the newspaper, glanced at the headlines, then tossed it aside and headed downstairs. Again, Jordan was front-page news with the prosecutor pushing toward getting the grand jury's vote for an indictment. If that happened, and he had little doubt it would, a second arraignment would be scheduled. A memorial for Steve Tanner was also on the horizon. He'd read that his children were planning an extravagant event to celebrate his life in rock 'n' roll history. All of those things were sure to keep the case in the public eye for a few more weeks.

The good thing about all the publicity, aside from the fact that it was forcing her to hide out in Water Mill, was that it was going to provide a good argument for a motion for a change of venue, though he doubted whether there was a place on earth where no one had heard of Steve Tanner. Still, even though it would be tough to impanel an impartial jury anywhere, one advantage to getting the trial moved to some out-of-the-way place was that it would make it a little easier to assure Jordan's safety.

"Looks like you're getting some work done," he said as he walked into the living room and observed her curled up on the sofa, tapping her fingers across the keyboard of her laptop. He strolled to a chair across from her and sat down.

"I'm trying to keep busy and not think about my case or that I'm probably the most hated woman in America."

"Is it working?"

"Somewhat. I'm searching for information about Steve and hoping that something will jog my memory, maybe loosen up the little bits of his life that he did reveal to me or that I saw. Maybe he told me something that I'd forgotten, or maybe I saw something that I thought was unimportant. Maybe there's a clue tucked somewhere in the back of my mind that will lead us to the murderer."

"From the look on your face, it doesn't appear that you've had any luck."

"No. I haven't."

"If there's anything you've missed, it'll surface." He stretched his arms over his head and settled his palms on the back of his neck. "And most likely when you least expect it. You'd be surprised at the types of things that can jog one's memory."

"I spent five weeks with him. One wouldn't think it would be that difficult."

"You're assuming the existence of something that may not exist." He felt the kick in his gut as he let his gaze glide down the length of her bare mile-long legs when she leaned back and slid them out from under her. He was beginning to question whether he had underestimated his ability to resist her, especially after the kiss on the beach. He'd known he'd enjoy it. In fact, he'd looked forward to it, but its impact had caught him by surprise. When she had pushed back, every muscle in his body had ached for more of her. "He may have never met the person who murdered him."

"Like a deranged fan?"

"That's a possibility. Occasionally, people don't know the person who murdered them."

"Oh, gosh. I never saw this photograph," she said, staring at the screen. "There's a picture of Steve and me together at an event. I wasn't aware we were being photographed. His arm's around me, and he's whispering to me. The caption says he was caught kissing his latest conquest and speculates that we might even be engaged." When she looked up from the computer, he saw the horror settle in her face. "How irresponsible to print something so untrue with absolutely no attempt to verify it. Anyone reading this might think it's true. A deranged fan who doesn't like the idea of him marrying someone might think it's true."

"On the other hand, more often than not, a murder victim knows the person who killed them. He could have been murdered by his recently discovered offspring. Maybe this person was jealous or resentful about being hidden all these years and being left out of the limelight."

She shook her head. "I think a deranged fan is more realistic. Behind Steve's impetuous, hard-partying lifestyle that the press managed to capture was a man of substance. That man, the press never depicted. He was kind and generous, and he adored all of his children. I just can't put any credence in a disgruntled illegitimate child theory. Given a chance, Steve would have done everything to make up for the years he'd lost with a son or a daughter." She looked down, closed her laptop, and lifted her gaze back to his. "How are we ever going to be able to find a deranged fan if that's who killed Steve? I overheard you on the phone tell someone that unless you find out who killed him, you aren't going to be able to get my case dismissed."

He heard enough pitch in her voice to know that she was more than a little worried. "First of all, I never said that I think

Tanner's murderer is a deranged fan." He lowered his arms and rested his elbows on the chair. "I'm saying that I'm not ready to rule out any theory. Secondly, it would make things a lot easier if we could find out who killed Tanner and get all the charges against you dropped. But your case is by no means a lost cause if we don't. We don't need to know who killed Tanner to get an acquittal. We need to put reasonable doubt in the jurors' minds about the prosecution's case." Of course, it wasn't as easy as he hoped he made it sound, but handling the trial and working the jury, if it came down to that, was his job. He didn't want her losing any more sleep over it than he was sure she was already. She needed to stay mentally and physically strong if she was going to get through this situation, and worrying herself sick wouldn't accomplish that.

"How will you convince a jury that I didn't kill Steve if you can't tell them who did?"

"There are many ways to do that, and you'll have to trust me when I say that I'm very good at it." Despite how good he was, however, there were always things beyond his control when it came to trials and juries, and that was why he wasn't giving up on finding out who had killed Steve. His investigator was already working on things.

"I'll try."

"There you two are," Mrs. Doyle said, appearing in the doorway. "I hope you're finished with work for the day. Dinner will be ready in about twenty minutes."

"Perfect timing," Reed said, tossing her a smile. "Just the thought of your cooking whets my appetite."

"Oh, dearie, you always did know what to say to warm a woman's heart," she said with a chuckle.

"Can I help you with anything, Mrs. Doyle?" Jordan asked.

"Not a thing, dear," she replied as she turned from the doorway.

"She certainly seems happy that you're here," Jordan said.

"And I have no doubt that she's just as happy to see you."

"Why? Is she lonely when you're not here?"

"Hell, no," he said and laughed. "If she ever was, she isn't anymore. She knows everyone in town. And in the next town over."

"Why would she care if I'm here, then?" She placed her laptop on the table.

"She's waiting for grandchildren. You were the closest I've ever come to getting married."

"You never married after we . . . after us?"

"I've been busy." She didn't need to know that it had taken him longer than he'd expected to get over her or that she wasn't easy to replace. "How about you?" he asked, but he knew the answer.

"No."

"Why not?"

She shrugged. "I don't know."

"My guess is that it isn't for lack of suitors."

"Do you ever turn off the charm?" The corners of her mouth lifted to a grin.

"I can't help it when I'm in the presence of someone who evokes it," he replied, meeting her grin.

"Well, that answers my question. I don't suppose there's a pair of hip waders in those bags upstairs?"

"Be nice, or I might have to have Mrs. Doyle remind you of just what a great guy I am."

As expected, the prosecutor had obtained a vote for an indictment, and the second arraignment had been scheduled for that morning. Reed had the security team tripled. He also had arranged for a decoy to accompany him from the courtroom after the hearing.

They arrived directly at the courthouse from Water Mill.

Reed was pleased with how seamless it all went. Jordan entered her plea of not guilty, and then they were out of there. The switch with the decoy went off flawlessly. No one had suspected that the woman tucked between Reed and one of the bodyguards he'd hired was one of the secretaries from his firm. Even the weather had cooperated. The rain had provided an excellent excuse for a prop. It was impossible to get a good look at the secretary past the umbrella that shielded her.

However, he was a bit less pleased when he arrived at his office afterward. "What the hell is going on in here?" he asked, scanning the mess in his office. The locks on his file cabinets had been pried out, some of the drawers had been left open, and a mountain of file folders and papers were scattered over the floor. Every drawer in his desk was pulled out, and his computer chassis was gone. A young police officer was bent over his credenza, dusting for fingerprints.

"Sir, I'm done with your desk, but don't touch anything else," he warned.

"We had a break-in during the night. I left you a voice mail on your cell phone," Rose explained, examining the tangle of cords strewn across his desk. "I'm sorry, I've been warned not to clean up anything until he's finished."

"Damn it." Reed dragged a hand through his hair and surveyed the damage. Then, looking at his cell phone, he realized he'd forgotten to turn it back on after the arraignment hearing. "How many computers did they get?"

"Just yours, sir," the officer replied without looking up. "Seems whoever did this was interested in something you have or something you know."

"Yours was the only office broken into," Rose said.

He was sure it had something to do with Jordan and Tanner. At the moment, none of his other cases had the possibility of implicating someone else in a murder. He was equally sure that the rookie cop sent on the call wasn't going to find out who had torn up his office. The kid hardly looked old enough to shave. He was probably sent as retribution for the countless times he'd made the department's officers look like bumbling Keystone Cops on the witness stand.

"Hopefully, the asshole won't be able to figure out my password or otherwise get past it." That would keep his other clients protected, not that he believed whoever stole his computer was interested in any of his other clients. And as far as Jordan was concerned, he had her physical file with him, and he hadn't yet had Rose transfer anything from his laptop to his desktop.

"I've set you up temporarily down the hall in the vacant office." Rose was already putting his desk back in order. "I'll forward all of your calls to you there."

"Thank you, Rose." He glanced at the young officer and shook his head on his way out. The kid was busy scooping a pile of spilled powder back into his powder jar. Reed had nothing at all against the police, it was just an unfortunate and necessary part of his job to point out when they didn't do their jobs well, and at the moment, he was glad he didn't have to rely on them. He had hired the beefiest guards at the agency to protect Jordan.

Jordan felt a little prick of guilt leaving Reed to fend off the herd of reporters and fans while she snuck out unscathed, but she hoped that with the police better prepared and the steady rainfall, things weren't as chaotic as they'd been after the first arraignment. She kept her fingers crossed that the rain had quieted things outside of her apartment, as well.

"Driver, we need to head toward Broadway and Houston," she said when they were a few blocks from the courthouse.

"We don't have time. We have a helicopter waiting for us

at the airport." The bodyguard next to her looked over the people along the street as he answered for the driver.

"I won't take long. Besides, isn't it a private helicopter that's waiting?"

"Yes, ma'am, it's Mr. Carrington's."

"Then we won't be holding anyone else up, and the pilot will have to wait for us if we're the only passengers. Besides, as I said, I won't be long."

"I'm sorry, Ms. Maxwell," the driver replied, glancing at her in his rear-view mirror. "I have instructions to drive straight to the airport."

"He's right, ma'am," the other guard concurred. "No deviations. Airport only. Those were our orders."

"Would those be Mr. Carrington's orders?"

"Yes, ma'am, they are. He is the one paying us."

"Well, as my attorney, Mr. Carrington works for me." She hoped a little logic might help persuade them. "He hired you on my behalf, and I'm the one that will be paying for your services, ultimately. So, you kind of answer to me."

The guards exchanged glances but were silent. She could tell they were thinking over what she said.

"Please?" A little begging may help, she thought. She looked out the window and checked the street signs. They weren't that far east yet. It wouldn't be that much of a detour if they turned south now. "It's not that far out of the way, and I'll be quick. I promise you won't get into any trouble with Mr. Carrington."

The guard checked his watch. "What is it you want to do?"

"I just want to pick up a few things from my apartment." If she was going to be stuck in Water Mill until after Steve's memorial event, she would need to get the passwords to her online accounts, not to mention pick up some extra clothes.

The driver looked over at the other guard. "It's up to you, man. I can pick up the speed so we won't lose that much time if we stop."

"All right," the guard relented. "But you're not leaving my side. Where you go, I go."

"Fair enough," she agreed. "And thank you."

"And leave the wig on."

A few turns and a few minutes later, they turned the corner to her street. She saw a couple of television vans and a handful of photographers loitering around her building, looking bored.

"That's my building, across from that white van," she said, pointing out one of the media vans.

"With the doorman?" The guard shook his head. "This won't work. He'll recognize you and tip off the vultures."

"No, he won't."

"I can guarantee you, he's already been paid off," he insisted.

"And I can guarantee you, he won't give me away."

"What makes you so sure about that?"

"Just take my word for it." Her voice held no room for doubt. "I'd stake my life on it."

"All right," he said, surveying the loiterers huddled under umbrellas and in doorways as they passed. "You better be sure about that."

"I am." And she was. The doorman had found out that she'd been responsible for saving his child's life, had gotten his child in to see the top pediatric cancer specialists, and had paid for everything not covered by his insurance plan. She had requested anonymity, but somehow he'd found out. He had called her a guardian angel, and she knew he would be hers when she needed one.

"Drop us off around the corner," he instructed the driver. "We'll draw attention if we get out here."

The driver nodded, turned at the next corner, and pulled to the curb. "I'll circle around. Call me when you're ready, and I'll pick you up out front."

"You'll hear from me in fifteen minutes," he said and pushed open the door. "Leave the umbrella here."

"But it's raining," Jordan replied.

"If they can't see you under an umbrella, they'll try for a closer look," he said, nodding in the direction of the photographers. "If they get an eyeful of your blonde hair, they might just ignore us."

She nodded, and as she stepped from the car, she pulled up the collar of the trench coat she had exchanged for her suit jacket with the decoy.

"Hold this as if you're shielding yourself from the rain and make sure it covers your face," the guard said, handing her a folded newspaper and slipping an arm around her. "I'll cover this side of you."

"Okay." She lifted the newspaper to her face. "I'm ready."

The guard gave two quick smacks to the car's roof, and the driver pulled into traffic. "It's just you and me now," he said as they took a few hastened strides and rounded the corner.

"Are they watching us?" she asked, trying to keep up with his pace. It felt like her feet were barely touching the ground with the grip he had on her and his quick strides.

"They're looking, but no one is making a move. Just keep your head down and the paper up."

She sensed people hurrying past them, and when she caught a glimpse of someone stopping in their path, she felt the guard's arm jerk around her. "Excuse me, you gotta light?" a man asked, fumbling with a rain-soaked cigarette.

"Don't smoke," the guard answered, pulling her past the man in one seamless move.

The driver's window on the television news van parked across the street from her building slid down, and she felt her breath hitch. It was all over, she knew it. The man with the

cigarette was the lookout. She was sure he was standing behind them, jumping up and down, signaling to the person in
the van.

"Keep your head down," the guard ordered.

She braced herself, waiting for the onslaught. She felt like
a rabbit surrounded by a pack of hungry wolves. Someone
was running toward them from the street. She could hear
their feet slapping against the wet pavement. Then she heard
a yell, followed by an angry horn and someone cursing.

"What was that?"

"Nothing," the guard answered.

"What about the van?"

"What about it?"

"I saw the window go down."

"They must've just needed air. No one has come out."

She released a slow breath, then heard a familiar voice.

"Good morning, miss. Sir." The doorman greeted them
with a friendly nod as he opened the door for them to pass.
Once inside, with a discreet wink, he resumed his position.
He was so nonchalant that she would have been sure he
hadn't recognized her if he hadn't offered the wink.

The lobby was empty, and they passed through it and into
one of the elevators without incident. She shook the water
from the drenched newspaper and tucked it under her arm
when the doors closed.

"How many units are on your floor?" the guard asked
when the elevator began its ascent.

"Four." Hers was the smallest at just under four thousand
square feet. But to her, it was enormous. She needed only
about a third of the space but had bought it because she loved
the cobblestone streets and cast-iron warehouses that dotted
the SoHo area.

"Which way are we heading off the elevator?"

"To the left. My apartment is the last door on the left. I

doubt we'll run into any of my neighbors. I'm sure they're not going anywhere in this weather."

"It's not your neighbors that I'm concerned about."

"I'm sure my doorman is being careful about who he is letting in the building."

"Hopefully, but it won't hurt to have your key ready."

"The key won't be a problem." At least it shouldn't be, she thought. Hers and the spare one Steve had given her to his apartment were still in his apartment as far as she knew. But she always kept a spare key to her apartment hidden in the hallway.

The doors slid apart, and he gestured for her to stay put while he stepped out and checked the hallway. "It's clear," he said, then stuck a foot on the threshold as the doors started to slide closed. The doors bounced back open when one hit his shoe.

She stepped out and headed down the hallway, stopping at a small light fixture hanging on the wall a few feet from her door. She dragged her fingers along the base of the fixture and felt for her key. It was where she had hidden it.

"That's not a good idea," the guard said, shaking his head.

"Why not?"

"It's too obvious."

She supposed he had a point, but when she had placed the key there, she'd been thinking more about convenience than safety.

The guard checked his watch as he closed the door behind them. "Ten minutes. Let me know if I can help you with anything."

"Thank you. I can manage." She tossed the newspaper on a glass table in the foyer, then peeled out of her wet trench coat. She carried it to the kitchen and draped it over the back of a chair. "There are drinks in the refrigerator. You can help yourself."

"I'm fine, thanks." He tugged the zipper down on his jacket and called after her as she hurried from the kitchen. "Don't turn on any lights, and stay away from the windows."

She hadn't thought about that, but with the natural light entering from the windows spanning the entire length of two sides of her apartment, there was no need to switch on any lights despite the cloudy day. As she passed her office, she glanced in, then stopped. Something seemed out of place, though she couldn't put her finger on it. It was probably just the fact that she hadn't been there for a while, she decided and continued toward her bedroom.

The bedroom looked just as she had left it. A silk robe was hanging on the hook of the open closet door, a pair of shoes was on the floor where she had stepped out of them, and a pair of jeans was lying across a chair. Aware of the time, she hurried into the bathroom and grabbed a few things. She carried them into her closet and dumped them into an overnight bag. She stuffed the bag with as much as it would hold and then changed into a pair of jeans and a blouse.

On her way back, she stopped in her office. As she moved the chair to her desk aside, it occurred to her that the chair was out of place. It had been placed under the desk. She always swiveled her chair toward the door when she got up and always left it in that position. That's odd that it's under my desk, she mused, but to think that someone has been in my home is ridiculous. Thieves don't tidy things up. A quick glance around confirmed that nothing seemed to be missing. She grabbed the disc on which she stored her passwords, picked up her bag, and headed back toward the kitchen. The phone rang as she set her bag back down.

"Don't answer it," the guard warned just as she was about to.

"It's Ernesto. From downstairs."

"The doorman?"

"Yes."

"How do you know?"

"By the ring tone."

"Let me answer it." He lifted the receiver. "Ernesto?"

Jordan saw annoyance flash across his face before he thanked Ernesto and replaced the receiver.

"Did you call someone named Charles while you were packing your things?"

"No. Why?"

"There's a Charles on his way up. Do you know him?"

"Yes. He's my friend."

"Here's your scarf," he said, shoving a red and black silk scarf into her hand and taking her bag. "We don't have time for social visits. I'm going to call Carl and have him meet us out front with the car in two minutes."

She looked down at the scarf. "Where did you get this?" It wasn't hers, and neither was the rich scent that emanated from it. A chill crept through her as she remembered the chair.

"I noticed it on the floor by the coffee table." He carried her bag to the foyer and set it down while he punched in the number for the driver. She grabbed her coat and followed him.

"That must be Charles," she said when they heard the knock at the door.

"Check whoever it is first, then I'll let him in if it's him."

He followed her to the door. She looked through the peephole, and when she nodded, he opened the door.

"Hi. I'm glad to see you're finally home," Charles said, stepping inside. He was drenched.

"Not for long. I'm afraid we were just leaving. This is my bodyguard."

He gave Charles a curt nod.

"Why are you leaving? Things seem to have settled down. There are a few newsmen out there, but it's pretty quiet."

"That's because they don't know I'm here. We snuck past

them on the way in." She slipped into her coat and stuffed the scarf in the pocket. "If anyone knew I was here, I'm sure the street would be swarming with reporters."

"Then why take a chance on them seeing you leave?"

"Reed thinks I shouldn't be here until after Steve's memorial event." And she was anxious, now, to get back to Water Mill and her laptop. The scarf made her theory of a deranged fan who didn't want to see him marry more likely than any of Reed's theories.

"Where are you going?"

"Water Mill." The words were out of her mouth before she realized that Reed probably didn't want him knowing where she'd be staying. It didn't matter, she decided. It wasn't like Charles was going to tell anyone.

"Let's go." The guard hoisted up her bag and slipped the strap over his shoulder.

"How will I get in touch with you? What if you need me?"

"Charles, you're so sweet." She gave his hand a squeeze. "And you're such a good friend. Don't worry about me. I'll call you if I need you, and I'll see you when I get back."

CHAPTER FIVE

"Your secretary told me I would find you in here. Some-one sure made a mess of your office."

Reed looked up as Congressman Gary Carr strutted into his temporary office wearing his classic pinstriped suit and spit-shined, laced-up wingtips, all screaming American-made. From his Pilgrim roots to his home in the suburbs with the *Cadillac* out front, he was as American as apple pie. Reed was well aware that he never let his constituents forget it or the bullet he had taken in Vietnam.

"Hello, Congressman." He stood, circled his desk, and extended a hand. He'd heard rumors that he would run for the presidency in the next election and wondered if they were true. "To what do I owe the pleasure?"

"Actually, I'm having lunch with Kent." He took his hand, gave it a crisp jolt, and lowered himself to one of the client chairs facing the desk. He folded his hands in his lap and sat ramrod straight. His posture and mannerisms reeked of the rank of major, leftovers from his military days, Reed guessed. "His secretary said he's on the phone, so I thought I'd stop in for a short visit."

"It's good to see you." He took a few strides back to his chair and sat down. "How's your boy doing?" The last time he'd seen his son was when he'd made the plea bargain with the district attorney's office. He'd gotten the charges for drunk and disorderly conduct dismissed in return for ten hours of community service. Lucky for Carr, he'd managed to keep the whole thing under the radar. He'd even gotten his son's record expunged after he had completed his community service. Nothing had ever hit the papers.

"He's doing well," he replied with a nod. "Thank you for asking. We won't be needing to call on you again, which is a good thing. It looks like you have your hands full these days."

"I'm keeping busy."

"So I hear. Steve Tanner's murder." He shook his head and released a whistle. "From what I've read, that's not going to be an easy one to defend."

"Murder cases are never easy to defend, especially when considering what's at risk."

"Do you think you'll be able to work out a plea for your client?"

He shrugged. "It's too early to tell."

"Looks like you're going to have to try, with all the publicity this case is getting."

"Sometimes publicity works in one's favor. It provides a good argument for a change of venue."

"I suppose, but your client's going to need more than that, isn't she? I heard they caught her practically red-handed."

"Things aren't always what they seem." He rocked back in his chair and studied the congressman. He wondered if maybe he sometimes wasn't what he seemed. Perhaps it was more than just idle curiosity that had Carr so inquisitive about Jordan's case. "Speaking of having hands full, I hear you're working on amending the waste bill. How's that coming?"

"It's coming along. We're ironing out some issues," he said, dismissing the topic. "Seems like a shame for your client to have to go through a trial." He frowned as he continued. "Her whole life is going to be put on display. I imagine every tawdry detail of her relationship with Steve Tanner will be made public."

It didn't take long for him to bring the conversation back

to Jordan, he thought. "What makes you think her relationship with Tanner was tawdry?"

He shrugged. "I'm assuming there was some reason, some ugly component of the relationship that led her to kill him."

"Let me ask you something, Gary." It was his turn to throw out a line to see what he could catch.

"Sure. Go ahead."

"Why are you so interested in this case? Or is it my client that you're interested in?" He kept his eyes on him and watched for a flinch. A twitch. The slightest indication of uneasiness.

Without a pause, he chuckled. "I must admit that I'm a bit embarrassed. I suppose I've gotten caught up in the sensationalism of it all. I think it's the closest thing New York's had to a scandal in a while."

He's smooth, he thought, but that's to be expected. The man is, after all, a politician.

"There you are, Gary. My secretary said you were wandering around here somewhere." Kent Willcox's voice trailed in from the doorway where he stopped to put on a suit jacket as dated as his Clark Gable mustache. He was one of the older partners in the firm, one who practiced on the wills and trust side. Reed had heard that he was a favorite among the widowed clients.

"I thought I would stop in on Reed for a few minutes." The congressman stood and extended a hand to Reed. "Good to see you again, Reed, and good luck with that case."

He stood and accepted the quick jolt of a handshake. "Good to see you, as well, Gary."

When he was sure he had left the firm's offices, he dialed Kent's secretary. "Mr. Wilcox's office, can I help you?" she answered.

"This is Reed. Can you tell me if Kent was on a call before he left for lunch?"

"No, not that I am aware of. It's been pretty quiet all morning on this side of the office."

"Okay, thanks." He set down the receiver and eased back in his chair. Carr had lied about Kent being on the phone. Maybe he had lied about getting caught up in the hype of it all, too, he pondered. Perhaps he did have something to do with Tanner's murder. No one was above suspicion, and he wasn't going to rule him out. At least not without a closer look. Right now, he didn't have much else.

Hell, he thought as he bounced forward and shoved aside a pile of paper. Maybe he was just grasping at straws with Carr. It was doubtful that a strait-laced right-wing WASP congressman would possibly have any connection to a wild, hard-partying rock star. He hoped he wasn't losing his perspective, his objectiveness. He had never represented a client with so much at stake for him personally. He had loved Jordan, and there was no way he could let her end up in prison. It was not an option. He had to get her acquitted. Period.

"Excuse me, Mr. Carrington?" Rose's voice spilled from the phone speaker.

"Yes, Rose."

"Your mother is on line one for you."

"Thank you. I'll take it." He released a long sigh. He knew why she was calling. He was just surprised it had taken her so long to find out about Jordan. He'd figured that with her circle of pretentious, pompous gossip-swappers, she would have known the day she'd been arrested. "Hello, Blair." Since he'd uttered his first words, his mother had insisted that he call her by name. *Mother* and any form of the word were much too dowdy for her tastes. He'd known that as far as she'd been concerned, she had fulfilled her maternal duties the moment he'd been born. She had produced an heir to carry on the Carrington name. The pregnancy and birth had been loathsome enough for her. Spit-up, dribble, sticky little hands, and the rest of raising a child she wasn't going to tolerate. That had been Mrs. Doyle's responsibility. "How are you today?"

"I'm fine. And you, darling?"

"Couldn't be better." He swiveled his chair around to face the window. Not being on a corner, that office didn't offer the Manhattan skyline that his did, but he took advantage of the view anyway.

"That's wonderful. I'm glad to hear that. And how is Mrs. Doyle? I understand you were in the Hamptons for a few days."

"Mrs. Doyle is as good as ever." He knew she didn't give a rat's ass about her. She'd never done anything for Mrs. Doyle in all her years of service other than paying her a salary. There had been no perks, no extra benefits. Nothing special was done for the woman who had raised her child. "What's on your mind?"

"I was at the salon today, and I heard an awful rumor. It simply cannot be true because your father hasn't mentioned a word about it to me."

"It's true, Blair." He was just going to cut to the chase. The sooner he had the conversation, the sooner it would be over, and he could get on with his day. "Jordan has been charged with murder, and I'm representing her."

"For heaven's sake, Reed. This just proves that everything I ever told you about that girl was true. She probably murdered that man because he refused to marry her. I'm lucky she didn't murder me for . . . for questioning whether she was good enough to be a Carrington. Why on earth are you getting yourself tangled up with her again?"

Questioning? That's putting it mildly, he thought. He'd already lost Jordan by the time he'd found out what his mother had said to her . . . before he could warn Jordan about his mother. Blair was not someone whose words one took to heart. In fact, she was quite the opposite. The way to survive her was to ignore what she had to say. Tell her as little as possible, let her rant, then get on with your day. He'd learned that lesson early in life. If you fell short of Blair's expectations, if you tried to argue with her, she'd hound you until you took your last breath. "It's just business, Blair. Nothing more. Jordan's not the first person charged with a murder that I've represented, and she won't be the last."

"Well, I'm glad to hear that. Just don't do anything you will regret."

"Wouldn't think of it." He knew exactly what he was doing, and this time, he would be the one to walk away.

"And is she paying you? You aren't doing this for, what do they call it, pro bono?"

"That's privileged information, Mother."

"Whatever. Just don't let her take advantage of you. I have to go, now. My masseur is here. *Ciao*, darling."

"You knew she would find out sooner or later," a familiar voice said from behind him.

He spun around and stared into the well-creased face of his father, who was making his way to one of the client chairs. At just sixty-five, Aldrich Carrington looked beyond his years and it made Reed wonder if it was due to the constant pummeling from Blair.

"I didn't hear you come in," he said, setting down the receiver. "How long have you been here?"

"Long enough."

"You didn't tell Mother about Jordan?"

"I have to live with her, son," he quipped.

"I can always represent Jordan outside of the firm," he offered.

"Wouldn't matter," his father replied, shaking his head. "Besides, from what I've heard, you'll need all the firm's resources for her case."

"That's true. This case isn't going to be any easier than any of the other murder cases I've handled."

"Especially with the personal stake you have in it."

"What are you talking about? It's been over five years since Jordan and I were together."

"I know what your plan is, son."

"My plan?" He cocked a brow.

"Come on. Are you going to make me spell it out? I know you've been using the firm's investigators to keep track of her for the past five years. I know you haven't had a serious relationship with a woman since Jordan. I know you went to her and offered her your representation. She didn't come to you. And you don't need to solicit clients." A smile cracked over his worn face. "And I figured Mrs. Doyle had a good reason to call me and tell me to make sure Blair kept out of your business this time around."

"Mrs. Doyle called you?"

"She's a pretty intuitive woman, it seems."

He sat back and met his father's smile. "Apparently." And more desperate for grandchildren than he thought. He considered for a second about setting his father straight and then decided against it. As long as his father stayed out of his way so he could accomplish what he wanted to accomplish, it didn't matter what his father thought his motivations were when it came to Jordan.

"Now, tell me what I can do to help you with her case."

"I don't know at this point. I'm trying to find out who had a motive to kill Tanner."

"You might want to expand your search." He lifted an elbow to the chair and rested his chin on his hand. "Find out who may have had a motive to kill Jordan. Maybe someone was trying to kill her, and Tanner got in the way."

"Why would you think that?"

"Turns out she's got a lot more money than what people think, son. Did you know that?"

"What makes you think that?"

"What do you think we estate planning lawyers do every month when we get together? Discuss the law? We talk about how much money is floating around this city."

"Are you telling me that Jordan's attorneys disclosed her personal finances to everyone at your monthly conference?" He didn't bother to conceal his irritation, although he was surprised by it since, as far as he was concerned, her wealth didn't change anything. "Isn't that a violation of their ethical obligations?"

"No, no, no. Calm down." He lifted his chin and gave Reed a dismissive wave. "It's not like that. Her attorney's Fred Braun. You know Fred. He and I go way back. He remembered you and Jordan had been engaged, and he mentioned to me, not everyone, just me, that she had come into a lot of money when her parents died. He was bragging about her, actually. Said she doesn't touch it. Doesn't need it. It just sits there. He said no one else gets a piece of it until Jordan dies. I thought that maybe someone is waiting in the wings, watching it just sit there and getting a little impatient."

"Hmm." He lifted a pen and slid it through his fingers as he mulled over his father's words. Maybe it was a possibility. He wondered who was entitled to her money if she died. "I don't know," he said, shaking his head. "If whoever killed Tanner intended to kill Jordan, he would have known she was in Tanner's apartment. Why wouldn't he have killed her, too?"

"Don't know. Maybe Tanner surprised whoever it was. He got spooked, killed Tanner, and ran."

"Maybe. It's worth considering." It gave him something more to go on than just Carr. "Maybe there is something you can check on for me."

"Just ask, son."

"Do you think you can find out who's handling Tanner's

estate?"

"I'm sure I can. Anything else?"

"See if you can find out what heirs Tanner named in his will and if he disinherited anyone. Also, if anyone asserts a claim as an unnamed heir, can you let me know?"

"No problem. Is that it?"

"For now, yes." He tapped his pen on the desk and paused for a minute. "And, Father, about Blair—"

"Good Lord, son. You don't know me at all, or you'd know you don't have to say it. If I told your mother anything, it would come back and bite me in the ass. And your mother certainly doesn't need me for information. She has a whole network of sources out there. Hell, she'll probably find out who murdered Tanner before you do."

"Sorry. I just know how relentless she can be at times. I'm sure she will be grilling you for information."

"It's nothing I can't handle with a few shots of Brandy. I've been married to the woman for over thirty-five years. I've gotten pretty good at tuning her out and dodging questions." He pushed himself up from the chair. "I'll let you get back to work. Make sure you let me know if there's anything else I can do to help. And keep me informed. I want to know what's going on and how it's going."

CHAPTER SIX

Jordan was still working on her first serving as she watched Mrs. Doyle flit around the kitchen. Mrs. Doyle had insisted on serving three full meals a day and refused to allow her to help prepare a meal or clean up afterward. She, in turn, had insisted that all their meals would be in the kitchen and that Mrs. Doyle would join her and her bodyguard. It was a bargain hard fought and not entirely won. Rarely did Mrs. Doyle sit down with them, except for dinner, and even then, she'd get up a few times during the meal to tend to something or other.

"That was really good, Mrs. Doyle. Thank you."

Jordan saw that the bodyguard had all but licked his plate clean. There wasn't a morsel left of the second generous helping of corned beef and cabbage that Mrs. Doyle had happily served up.

"You could spoil a man real fast with meals like this every night."

"A nice young man like you has to be married," Mrs. Doyle said as she pulled a pie out of the refrigerator. "Doesn't your wife cook, Ben?"

"Yeah, but not every night. We're both working a lot of hours right now." He pushed back from the table and scooped up his plate. "We're trying to save up to buy a house."

"No, you don't," Mrs. Doyle reminded him. "Put that down." She placed the pie on the table and took Ben's plate. She set it aside and sat down. "You're not finished yet. There is still some apple pie left from last night."

"Oh, no. I can't." He stood up, then slid his chair under the table. "I didn't leave room. But I'll sure have some later." He looked over at Jordan.

"I'll catch up," she said with a nod and a smile. They'd been in Water Mill for three days after the second arraignment and had already established a routine, at least after dinner. Ben would check the other buildings on the property, then she'd join him on his walk as he checked out the rest of the grounds. It was a nice distraction at the end of the day, and she looked forward to it.

"That young man eats so fast it's a wonder he even tastes his meal," Mrs. Doyle remarked after he had left. She took the last bite of cabbage on her plate, then got up again and waddled toward the stove when the tea kettle started to scream.

"It looked to me like he enjoyed it," Jordan said. "I don't see how he could not. You're a wonderful cook."

"That's because I enjoy eating," she said with a chuckle. "Would you like a cup of tea?"

"No, thank you." She took another bite and swore she could feel her waistline expand with it. She was sure that with Mrs. Doyle's cooking and the massive portions she served, she wouldn't leave Water Mill without a few extra pounds. But she was going to need them if she couldn't find out who killed Steve and would be eating dinner in prison every night. She just hoped that Reed was making some progress while in the city.

"Can I get you anything, dear?" Mrs. Doyle asked when she returned with her cup of tea.

"I'm fine." She shook her head. "Please sit and enjoy your tea."

"So, tell me, do you have a man in the city that looks out for you?"

Jordan half smiled and raised a brow. "Are you asking me if I'm dating someone?"

"I'm just wondering if you have a man in your life." She took a noisy slurp of tea but kept her gaze on Jordan. "A pretty young lady like yourself ought to have a man in her life."

"So, unlike the rest of the world, you don't believe I was dating Steve Tanner?" According to the newspapers and gossip columns, it seemed to be a foregone conclusion.

"Of course not." She laughed, and when she did, her whole body shook and her cup of tea with it. She dabbed a napkin over the splash that had landed on her apron. "I don't believe a word about that. I know it's all blarney."

"I hope there are more people like you out there." She was going to need them to be on her jury. "Even Reed believed I was dating Steve, at first."

"That's because the little green-eyed monster had a hold of him."

"What?" It was her turn to laugh now. "Mrs. Doyle, Reed and I haven't been together for a long time. We haven't even seen each other for five years."

"That may be so," she said, taking another gurgling sip. "But I think I know my Reed."

"I can assure you, our relationship is strictly professional," she insisted.

"I've seen the way you two look at each other." With a nod and a wink, she added, "It isn't strictly professional."

Recalling what Reed had said about Mrs. Doyle wanting grandchildren, she smiled. That's what this is all about, she thought. "I hate to disappoint you, but I'm afraid you're reading more into the situation than is there." She was sure the only thing Reed felt for her was maybe some sense of fondness because they had a history together and perhaps a sense of obligation to do what he could to keep her from going to prison. As for her, the only thing she felt for Reed was gratitude and hope that he might manage to get her out of the mess she was in. Of course, she couldn't deny the physical attraction, but it was nothing more than that, and that wasn't love.

"I'm not disappointed, dear. I know you have other important things to think about right now." She set her cup of tea on the table. "Are you sure you won't have a piece of pie?"

"I'm too full right now, but I would love to have a piece later." She stacked her plate on top of Ben's, gathered the silverware, and then set it on top. "That was a delicious meal. Thank you."

"Jordan, are you finished eating yet?" Ben asked, popping his head through the doorway after finishing his first round.

"Perfect timing." In more ways than one, she thought. The conversation had gotten too personal, and she didn't enjoy dashing the poor woman's hope for grandchildren. "I just finished." She pushed her chair from the table and stood. "Are you sure I can't help you with the dishes, Mrs. Doyle?" she asked.

"Absolutely not. Go. I'll put this pie back in the refrigerator so you two can have it later."

"All right. Thank you for dinner, then," she replied and headed outside.

By the time they had finished their walk, Mrs. Doyle had cleaned the kitchen and retired to her cottage. She had left a note on the center isle reminding them about the apple pie. Jordan had still been too full from dinner and had left Ben to enjoy the pie by himself. With the arraignments over, the stress of waiting for the trial was beginning to wear on her.

She sat on the bed, her legs crossed, the smooth silk of the scarf falling in her lap as she turned it over, examining it. The pattern was beautiful, the fabric exquisite. It was a *Ferragamo*, definitely high-end. She lifted it to her face and filled her lungs with the perfume scent that still clung to it. It was rich and sophisticated, and she imagined that the woman who wore it was, too. She couldn't imagine how it had gotten into her apartment and why whoever it belonged to had been there. She wondered what the woman had been looking for and whether there was a connection between her and Steve.

She had scoured the web, examining every photograph of Steve Tanner she could find. There had been thousands of them, and she had hoped to see the scarf in one of them. Scads of women had been photographed draping themselves around Steve, but none had been wearing the scarf.

A piercing ring from the nightstand broke the silence, startling her. She grabbed the receiver and answered the call. Reed's deep voice floated through her like a ribbon of warmth. It was comforting to hear his voice. It's nothing more than that, she told herself. After all, he had kept her out of jail and was working on keeping her out of prison.

"How was your day?" he asked. "Are you still hanging in there?"

"If you call sitting around feeling helpless hanging in there, then yes. I feel like I should be doing something to help myself."

"There's nothing for you to do at this point but stay safe. Have you been able to do any writing? Maybe that will help you keep your mind off of things."

"I've tried, but I keep losing my concentration."

"I should be able to get enough done here to make it back tomorrow. I should be there before dinner. We can talk more then."

"Good. I was wondering when I would see you again." She needed to tell him about the woman who had been in her apartment, show him the scarf, and discuss their next steps to plan her defense.

"Well, it's nice to know you're missing me." She could hear the ribbing in his tone, and she didn't need to see the grin to know it was there.

"Oh, yes. Be still, my beating heart," she quipped.

"I'll see you tomorrow," he replied, ignoring the sarcasm.

She settled the receiver in the cradle but snatched it up again. Talking to Reed had been a pleasant diversion, nothing more. The little flutter in her heart meant nothing, and she dialed the number to *Between the Pages* to prove it.

"*Between the Pages*," a raspy voice answered.

She recognized Herman's voice. They had never been introduced, but she'd seen him occasionally at the store, and he'd always seemed irritated about something. She had asked Charles once why he didn't have a talk with Herman about being so rude, but he'd just mumbled something about not having to pay him much and seemed reluctant to discuss the subject, so she never brought it up again.

"Hello, may I speak with Charles, please?" she asked, trying to sound polite. She heard a grunt, then a thud when the receiver was dropped. After a couple of minutes, she heard someone lift the receiver.

"This is Charles."

"Charles, it's Jordan. I hope I didn't catch you at a busy time."

"A little," he answered. "Are you home? I can call you back."

"No, I'm not home yet, but I wanted to talk to you. Do you have a couple of minutes?"

"You're still in Water Mill?" There was a hint of annoyance in his voice, and it made her think he was busier than just a little.

"Look, we don't have to talk now. I can call you back tonight after you're finished working and after the book club meeting." Wednesday nights were the book club meetings at *Between the Pages*, and she knew he always had to do a few things to prepare for them.

"Yeah. That's a good idea. I'll be able to talk to you as long as you want then."

"All right. Around ten?"

"Perfect," he answered and hung up.

After a few hours, she called him back. The meeting had broken up, and he sounded more relaxed than earlier.

"So, is your lawyer making any progress with your case?" he asked.

"I don't know. He's been in the city for the past few days, but he'll be back here tomorrow. I guess I'll find out then."

"He's going to be staying with you?"

"Well, yes. This is his home."

"I thought you were staying at some safe house or something like that, somewhere he sends all his clients who need to hide out."

"I think he considers this place safe. I don't know how many other clients he's sent here to hide, but I'm the only one right now."

"How long before you come home? Some of the book club members were asking about you, you know, since I know you. They want the inside story on what's going on."

"I don't know when I'll be going home. I'm hoping things will calm down after the tribute put together for Steve."

"Oh, yeah. That's supposed to be a pretty big deal. It's unbelievable," he said. "A guy like that dies, and suddenly, he's being honored like he's some hero or something."

She found herself frowning at the remark. "What do you mean by that? Steve Tanner was very accomplished in his career."

"C'mon, Jordan. Career?" He chuckled. "What he did wasn't work. It was play. Every time the man stepped on stage, I'll bet he was stoned out of mind."

"Maybe, but he was extremely talented, and millions of people love his music."

"Yeah, but it's not like he saved lives or did something remarkable for mankind."

"He was a kind and generous man, and every time he performed, he brought joy to people. He deserves recognition for his talent and the kind of man he was, whether you think so or not."

"I think not." A hint of sarcasm entered his voice. "And had you not been so enamored with him, you would think not, too."

"I wasn't enamored with him." If she didn't know Charles better, she would think he was jealous. Of course, it wouldn't necessarily be unreasonable. She hadn't stopped in the book store or talked to Charles the entire time she'd been staying with Steve. It had been all-consuming getting to know him and his family and friends and gathering information for his biography.

"Well, that's not what was being reported. And listen to yourself. The guy gets killed, you're blamed for it, and you're still all gaga over him."

"I am not gaga over Steve Tanner. I just think that he's a wonderful person who's had an exceptional career and deserves to be honored." And she did not enjoy having to defend him to Charles. "Look, I didn't call you to argue."

"I'm sorry. I know you have enough to deal with. I guess I shouldn't have taken that dig."

"It's all right. I have to go, anyway. I'd like to get some sleep so I can try and get some writing done tomorrow." She hung up and lay back against the pillows. Charles certainly hadn't proved her point.

Her husband's hand landed hard against the side of her head, nearly knocking her from the chair and scattering the mail Victoria had been going through all over the floor. She hadn't expected the blow even though it was not the first time he'd raised a hand to her. Gary Carr always knew just where to strike so that his assault would leave no marks, no evidence, and no visible trace of the punishment he dispensed.

"You stupid cunt!" He spat out the words, his voice reeking with rage and disgust. Victoria Carr lifted a hand to ward off the second blow as she struggled to blink away the tiny flashes of light that danced across her vision. She wasn't quite quick enough, and a sharp pain shot through her back as a second slap slammed against her throat, forcing her shoulder blade to smash against the back of the chair.

"Stop, please," she managed as she pushed herself out of the chair and out of striking range.

"If I lose the nomination next year because of you, you can bet you will pay!"

"I thought you were going to talk to Reed Carrington? He couldn't have told you anything. I know she doesn't know." She took a step back to widen the distance, the pain in her back still raw, the fear in her eyes sharp enough to mask the sadness that lived behind them.

"He didn't tell me a goddamn thing. If she knows, it will come out, and if it comes out—" He took a step toward her, but she was quicker this time. She spun around and ran from the room before he could deliver the next hit.

She rushed up the winding staircase, her fingers skimming along the smooth, wood railing. At the top of the stairs, she turned and hurried to the last suite at the end of the floor. It was the farthest suite from the one she had once shared with her husband. Inside, she knew she was safe. For some reason that she never questioned, but for which she was grateful, Gary Carr never entered her suite.

She walked to her closet and slid the pocket doors apart just enough to slip inside. She stepped out of her shoes, and her feet sank into the thick, plush carpet. There was a section of cedar-lined drawers at the far end of the closet. She walked over and slid open the bottom drawer. She removed a box and took it with her to the round bench in the center of her closet. She sat down, opened the box, and unwrapped the soft cloth around a simple, gold picture frame.

She stared at the faded photograph for a long moment, then placed it close to her heart. A tear slid down her cheek. She didn't bother to brush it aside, and it fell onto her hand.

Chapter Seven

"So far, we've checked birth records for New York," Harry Connor, one of the firm's investigators, reported. He was a big, burly man and didn't hesitate to use intimidation, if necessary, to get the answers he wanted. That was one of the reasons Reed had chosen him to help him with Jordan's case. "We've come up dry. The only records with Tanner listed as the father during and after his marriages are for the three children we already know about."

"Find out every state he toured across for the past thirty years and check the birth records for those states," Reed instructed. "And if he toured outside of the country, check the records in those countries, as well."

"I'll get right on it." He jotted down a few notes, then continued. "I also checked the court records for the past ten years. Tanner had a restraining order issued about five years ago against some lunatic minister stalking him."

"Where's the minister now?"

"Don't know. I'm still working on tracking him down."

"See if you can talk to any of the guys in Tanner's band. Find out how they felt about him and if they know of anyone who might want to see him dead. And, see if you can find out if he had any other stalkers that he hadn't gotten restraining orders against. Maybe he had a stalker that he didn't take seriously enough." Reed glanced at his *Cartier* watch, a gift he'd bought to cheer himself up after Jordan had left him. He figured he'd have enough time to finish up with Harry and still make it to Water Mill in time for dinner.

"I'll see what I can do. They might not be too excited about talking to someone on the alleged killer's team. I might have to get creative."

"Pull out all the stops on this case, Harry. Money is not a problem." He leaned back in his chair and continued. "What about Gary Carr? Have you found any connection between him and Tanner?"

"None, but I'm still digging. The congressman's either real clean or good at covering his tracks. I haven't found so much as a traffic ticket on the guy."

"He's had his eye on running for the presidency. If he's covered up anything, it'll be under layers. Dig deep." His gut was telling him that Carr was worth a closer look. He'd been just a little too anxious to talk to him and just a little too curious about Jordan's case. "Did you find anything on the cameras at the club the night he was murdered?"

"No. There was nothing suspicious on the cameras. No one hanging around looking like they were stalking him. And none of the employees noticed anything out of the ordinary. What about Tanner's kids? Want me to contact them, check them out? And what about the actress Tanner had his last kid with?" He looked down at his notes. "Claire Richards, that's her name. Want me to check her out?"

"Yes. Throw the net wide. We're trawling right now." Reed stood and took a few steps. He always thought better on his feet. "See if Tanner's building had a doorman. If so, talk to him. Ask him who Tanner came and went with, and ask him if Tanner had any disputes with his neighbors." He took a few more strides, then stopped. "See if you can find out what other bars and clubs Tanner frequented. Talk to the employees there and see if they can tell you anything. And see if there were any civil suits filed against Tanner over the past ten years. Maybe you can find a disgruntled manager or someone else who was unhappy with Tanner."

"Got it." He flipped over the page on his pad. "What about your client?"

"I'll concentrate on her. I want you to concentrate on everything else."

He nodded. "Anything or anyone else you'd like me to talk to or check out?"

He thought and mulled over whether to let it slip to the public that Jordan was planning to write Tanner's biography. Even with Tanner dead, she was unwilling to violate his trust, and she'd be furious if he did. He was willing to take the risk, though, even if she wasn't. It might bring something out of the woodwork. But the timing wasn't right, yet, he decided. "No. Not right now." If he was going to do something that would piss Jordan off as much as leaking the biography was sure to, he'd be damn sure it would get him results.

"Okay. I'll call you in a couple of days and let you know how I'm progressing," Harry replied and extended a rough hand to Reed.

"I'll wait to hear from you." Reed took his hand and returned the solid shake. "If anything comes up before, then, call me."

"Will do," he replied and strode from the room.

Reed tapped the intercom button on his phone, and Rose's voice answered. "Yes, Mr. Carrington."

"Rose, can you call the pilot and let him know I'll be ready to leave in about thirty minutes?"

"Certainly, sir. I'll let him know."

"Thank you." He picked up the newspaper lying on his desk since that morning and glanced at the front page. There was a blurb about Jordan that was reported at length in another section of the newspaper. He flipped to the page and stared at the picture. It was his and Jordan's engagement photograph. The corner of his mouth lifted as he stared at her. He didn't have to read the article to know what it was about. He closed the paper and tossed it on the pile of other newspapers with articles on her and the case.

He strolled over to the wall of windows spanning the south side of his office and peered out at the jungle of buildings. Clouds were moving in over the city, and it was beginning to sprinkle.

Overcast and drizzling for the better part of the day, it should have been a perfect day for writing. However, early on, Jordan had given up trying to work. She spent most of the day on the Internet searching, again, for some clues to solving Steve Tanner's murder. It was worse than trying to find a needle in a haystack. She had no idea what she was looking for and just hoped she would recognize a clue if she saw one.

By late afternoon, the rain had started to come down hard, and she wondered if Reed would make it back to Water Mill. She was disappointed at the possibility that he might not. She'd been anxious all day to find out if his investigator had uncovered anything useful. She also couldn't wait to tell Reed about the woman who had been in her apartment and the scarf she had left. Her gut told her that whoever she was, she had to have something to do with Steve's murder.

There was no way to tell him about the scarf without telling him that she'd persuaded Ben and the other bodyguard to deviate from his instructions to go directly to the airport from the courthouse. But she'd make sure they didn't get in trouble. She'd promised them that, and besides, she'd grown fond of Ben. And considering that she ate two of her three meals every day with him, she didn't want him mad at her.

Neither Mrs. Doyle nor Ben had called her to come down for dinner by six o'clock. She'd spent almost the entire day cooped up in her suite and decided she needed a change of pace. She closed the lid on her laptop, set it on the nightstand,

and headed downstairs.

As she strolled down the stairs, she thought she heard Reed's voice, and when she entered the kitchen, she was surprised to see he'd made it back despite the rain. She'd thought for sure he was going to wait out what looked like to be the beginning of a full-blown storm.

He looked as if he'd walked off the pages of a men's fashion magazine in the double-breasted dark gray designer suit he was wearing, and it made her wish she'd at least brushed her hair and put on a swipe of mascara.

"It's getting pretty wet out there," he explained to Mrs. Doyle. He lifted the foil off a bowl on the counter and peeked inside. "I think the storm's coming up from the south."

"I'm glad to see you made it here before the worst of it hits," Mrs. Doyle told him.

"I figured I better get here before you girls get too used to Ben being around here," he said with a wink in Jordan's direction.

"Don't go worrying about that. You'll always be my favorite boy, dearie," Mrs. Doyle said. "Now go get changed," she ordered, shooing him from the kitchen, "before you get something on that fancy suit. Dinner's just about ready."

"All right," he replied, snatching a piece of celery off the counter. "You're looking lovely this evening," he said to Jordan on his way out. "I think Water Mill agrees with you."

"I can't complain. Where's Ben?" she asked after Reed had left.

"Reed relieved him. Told him the pilot said he could take him back to the city tonight if they left right away." She tapped the spoon on the rim of the pot she had been stirring, then set it down. "He said to tell you goodbye and that he would see you next week. That Ben's such a nice young man. He sure did take his guarding of you serious. Always out walking around, getting to know the property."

"Yes, he is nice, and I think he was beginning to miss his wife." Noticing that the kitchen table was not set, she strolled over to the cabinet where the dishes were kept and reached for three plates. "I feel bad about that."

"The table's already set, dear. I'll be serving you and Reed in the dining room." She pulled a baking dish out of the oven and placed it on the center counter. "You shouldn't feel bad about that. I'm sure it's the nature of his job. And I'm sure it beats getting shot at any day."

"I don't think I can argue with that." She knew better than to ask Mrs. Doyle if she could help with anything else. "But I'm sure he's looking forward to seeing his wife."

"He probably is. Men need wives." She glanced up from slicing a loaf of bread, caught Jordan's gaze, and then finished. "You can take my word on that."

She smiled at Mrs. Doyle's not-so-subtle hint. She had been pelting her with them since she'd arrived. She'd tried to convince Mrs. Doyle that there was no possibility of her and Reed getting back together, and every time, Mrs. Doyle would just nod and tell her that she and Reed couldn't fight what the Good Lord had in mind.

"Now, dear, you go and tell Reed not to dawdle. I've held dinner for as long as I can."

"All right," Jordan replied. "I'm on it."

She could hear Reed whistling from the top of the stairs, and she followed it down the hall. He'd left the door to his suite open, and when she walked in, he was stepping out of a closet wearing just a pair of jeans. Her pulse stuttered before it kicked into lightning speed as she took in the ripples of fine-toned muscle.

She let her gaze linger while he strode toward an armoire, and she hoped that the flush of heat hadn't reached her cheeks. He pulled out a t-shirt, and she watched him unfold it. She knew he hadn't seen her yet as she watched his muscles flex when he slid the shirt over his head. Every movement tested her resolve to keep their past behind them.

When he started toward the door, he noticed her and a smile crossed his face. "I take it dinner's ready?"

"It is," she replied as she took a slow breath, fortified her resolve, and met his smile. "And it's my responsibility to make sure you don't dawdle."

"Then, shall we?" He took her arm, tucked it through his, and led her down the stairs to the dining room.

Smoldering flames in votive candles flickered among the red rose petals scattered across an elegant, white, lace tablecloth. Two place settings of fine china with a delicate gold and navy pattern graced the table. Wine had already been poured into two crystal glasses, and the Righteous Brothers' *Unchained Melody* played in the background. Well done, Mrs. Doyle, he thought. This will work to my benefit.

He pulled a chair out for Jordan, and as he took his seat, Mrs. Doyle waltzed through a doorway that led from the kitchen. She guided a silver cart loaded with various serving dishes to the table.

"Whatever you have there, it smells heavenly," he remarked, glancing at the cart. "I think you just may have outdone yourself this time."

"I hope you like it," she said, placing each dish on the table. After she set down the last one, she returned to the kitchen.

"Reed, you've got to talk to Mrs. Doyle about this," Jordan whispered. "She's got to stop."

"About what?" He cocked an innocent brow and the corners of his mouth lifted. "Her cooking?"

"You know what I mean. She's getting her hopes up that we'll get back together. She's been making innuendos to me since the day I arrived."

"God bless her little heart," he said with a grin. He knew Mrs. Doyle well enough to know that once she made her mind up about something, there was no stopping her. She was likely hell-bent on getting them back together, and he had no intention of interfering in whatever she had up her sleeve.

"No, not bless her little heart. She's going to be terribly disappointed when it doesn't happen."

"Jordan." He lifted her glass of wine and handed it to her. "Mrs. Doyle is a grown woman. She can handle disappointment." He lifted his glass and tapped it against hers. "Let's just relax and enjoy this incredible meal that she's prepared for us."

"All right, but her disappointment will be on your hands," she warned and took a sip of wine.

"I accept full responsibility for Mrs. Doyle's disappointment," he replied. "If that makes you feel any better."

Pushing back through the door, Mrs. Doyle asked, "Can I get you two anything else?"

"No. This is perfect," Reed answered. "But I'd like you to take the rest of the night off so I know you're safe in your bungalow before the weather gets any worse."

"I still have dessert to serve," she replied. "And the dishes to wash."

"Jordan and I can serve ourselves dessert, and we're more than capable of cleaning up after dinner."

"Well, the rain does sound like it's starting to come down a little harder, but I don't want you to lift a finger cleaning up anything," she replied. "The dishes can sit until the morning. I'll take care of them then."

"Don't worry about the dishes, Mrs. Doyle," Jordan replied. "I'll put them in the sink and let them soak."

"Well, okay," she agreed. "I'll just finish putting the pots and pans away, and then I'll be on my way. You two darlings enjoy your evening." She retreated into the kitchen.

A flash of lightening sparked outside the window, followed by a roaring clash of thunder. "It sounds like you made
it here just in time," Jordan said, lowering her glass of wine.
"I hope Ben makes it back to the city safely. I sure wouldn't
want to be out in that."

"He's in competent hands. He'll be fine. There's a car at the
airport. He can drive back to the city if my pilot thinks it's too
dangerous to fly." He offered her a piece of bread and then
took one himself. "Speaking of Ben, he tells me you took a
detour the other day from the courthouse."

"He told you about that?"

"He works for me." The corners of his lips turned up. "So,
he reports to me."

"You didn't give him a hard time about it, did you? I made
him take me to my apartment. I really didn't give him a
choice. And he was extremely careful, extremely protective.
He made sure there were no—"

"No," he interrupted as he served her a slice of roast. "I
didn't give him a hard time. After all, I work for you, and you
will ultimately be paying his bill." A grin formed across his
face as he lowered the serving fork, leaned back in his chair,
and settled his gaze on her. "Isn't that right?"

"Well, I had to come up with something to convince him to
deviate from your instructions, and . . . it is true. In any event,
thank you for not giving him a hard time."

"That doesn't mean that I'm not going to give you a hard
time." He took a drink of wine and then continued. "It's not
only crazed Tanner fans I'm concerned about when it comes
to your safety. Until we find out why Tanner was murdered
or who murdered him, we can't be certain your life isn't in
danger. And until we're certain of that, you have to take your
safety seriously and let the guards do their jobs."

"You're right, and I will."

"I'm glad you agree." He lifted a bowl of potatoes and held

them while she scooped a spoonful onto her plate. "And let me remind you, I'm running the show. What I say goes. I don't want to have to worry about interference from you."

"I understand, but it turned out to be good that we went by my apartment."

"How's that?"

"Someone was in my apartment."

"I know. Ben told me Charles came there." He took a bite of the roast. "I was right. I think Mrs. Doyle has outdone herself. And, I don't see Charles as a good thing. How did he know you were there, anyway?"

"I don't know. Maybe he saw us get out of the car." She swallowed a forkful of potatoes. "Mm. I have to agree about Mrs. Doyle. His bookstore is across the street from where Ben and I got out to walk to my apartment, but I'm not talking about Charles. Someone else was there."

"Who? Ben didn't mention that anyone else was there."

"Ben doesn't know." Another angry clash of thunder roared outside as she took a drink of wine and then continued. "Someone had been there before we got there. Someone had come into my apartment while I was gone."

"How do you know?" He was sure Ben would've noticed if her apartment had been ransacked and would've told him. "Were things missing?"

"I don't know. I wasn't there long enough to notice if anything was taken. The only thing I noticed was that the chair in my office was pushed under my desk. I always leave it turned, facing the door."

"Is that the only thing that was disturbed? That's why you think someone had been there?"

"No. I'm not finished. Before we left, Ben handed me a scarf that he said was lying by the coffee table. He thought it was mine. But it isn't. Whoever was in my apartment left it there."

"Are you sure it doesn't belong to one of your friends?"

"I've never seen it before, and I don't recognize the perfume on it."

"Did you bring it with you?" It could be the first break in the case, he thought. But he knew better than to get too excited about it. He wasn't one to put all his eggs in one basket, and he didn't want to raise any false hopes for Jordan. They had a scarf, not a suspect.

"Yes. It's upstairs."

A flash of lightening drew his attention, and he thought he saw a figure just outside the window. He pulled his phone from his pocket, got up, and strolled to the window. "Excuse me. I'm going to check on Mrs. Doyle," he said as he punched in her number and, looking outside, scoured the grounds. "I'm just checking to make sure you made it to the cottage all right," he said into the phone. Satisfied Mrs. Doyle was safe, and seeing no one outside, he walked back to the table. He activated the security system from his phone, then tucked it back in his pocket.

"Is she safely inside?" Jordan asked when he sat back down.

"Yes." He nodded. "No worries."

"Good."

"You were telling me about someone else being in your apartment. When you went to your apartment, did you notice any signs of forced entry? Was the area around the key slot scratched or the door jamb scraped?"

"No. I opened the door myself. I didn't notice any damage."

"Would your doormen have let anyone in your apartment?"

"Definitely not. Never without my permission."

"What about in the case of an emergency?"

"Someone would try to get in touch with me first, and I'd

be told in any event."

"If someone had been there, how would they have gotten entry?"

"I don't know." She shrugged. "It's possible someone knew where I hid my spare key."

"Any ideas who that could be?"

"No." She shook her head.

"All right. I'm going to need the scarf." He was going to send it out for DNA analysis. Hopefully, if there was DNA on it, it could be matched up with someone. "And, I'm going to need the names of your doormen and concierge."

"Of course." She nodded.

"I think you should come back to the city with me. We'll go to your apartment. I'll talk to your doormen and the concierge, and you can go through your apartment to see if anything is missing."

"Okay, and I'd like to talk with the investigator."

"I'll call him and set up a meeting if I haven't heard from him when we're ready to go back." He lifted his glass and stared at her face in the dim light of the candles. No more business, he decided. There would be plenty of time to discuss the congressman and the terms of Jordan's inheritance before they went back. Besides, it would be a shame to waste the wine and the candles on discussing work. "Do you think you can let yourself take a break from everything and enjoy the rest of the evening? We can start fresh tomorrow."

"I think so." A rumble of thunder exploded outside, and the lights flickered. "It doesn't sound like the storm intends to let up," she said.

"No, it doesn't. How do you like the wine?"

"I like it. It's a Merlot. My favorite. I suppose you remembered that, too?"

"Some things you don't forget. How about joining me in another glass before we have dessert?"

"That would be lovely."

He sliced the foil under the lip of a new bottle and peeled it off. Then he inserted the corkscrew and eased out the cork. He remembered how he had just as easily removed her clothes, more than once, a long time ago, and allowed the thought to linger. He filled her glass and handed it to her. She lifted it to her lips, and he watched as she let her gaze wander over him, sure she shared his thoughts.

A streak of lightening jetted across the window just outside, followed by a violent clash of thunder. The rest of the house went dark, and the music quieted. The candles on the table provided the only flickers of light, the torrent of rain the only sound. He stared at her in the dim light. It was easy to get lost in her, and it was beginning to get just as difficult to ignore the emotional pull as it was the physical pull.

"I think we lost power," she said over the rim of her glass.

"So it would seem." Not that it matters, he thought as his gaze followed the line of her jaw, the length of her neck. He remembered what it was like to drag his fingers down that neck, to feel her flesh under his fingers. To feel her heart beat against his. He'd known he'd have to deal with the physical attraction. Hell, he'd been looking forward to it, although he hadn't counted on it being so damn fierce. He resisted the urge to reach over and touch her, but the tension in his gut told him he was fighting a losing battle.

He looked away, but just for a moment. He angled his chair toward her, leaned back, lifted his glass, and settled his gaze on her once more. He took a drink and watched her take another, then lick the wine from her lips. He remembered how those lips had once tasted.

She met his gaze, and he held it. He could still read her mind regardless of how much time had separated them. He knew that despite her insistence to stay out of the past, she was slipping back, and her eyes told him that she wasn't re-sisting.

He took a generous swallow, then set his glass down. The circumstances couldn't be better. The timing couldn't be more perfect. It was time to take her back. It was time to remind her what she had walked away from.

He pushed his chair back and stood. He took a step toward her and set his hand on the back of her chair. When she lowered her glass to the table, he took her hand and pulled her up to him so close he could feel their passion collide. In an instant, their desire to visit the past obliterated any vows to avoid it.

He covered her mouth with his before she could take her next breath. He could taste her hunger. It rivaled his own. It was ravenous, insatiable. He tore at her shirt, not caring if it ripped to shreds, desperate to feel the warmth of her flesh underneath. It was like velvet under his fingers, and its softness made his blood simmer. He explored every exposed inch of her, greedy for more.

He jerked his shirt over his head and threw it aside. Raw nerves sizzled on every part of his body touched by hers. He was consumed by need, frenzied and primal. He wanted to devour her whole, every delicious inch of her.

The urgency spiked when he pulled at the snap of her jeans, then yanked at the zipper. His mouth was on hers again, his hands sliding down the curves of her waist to her hips. She wrestled with the button on his jeans, her hands trembling in the wildness of it all. He jerked when she pulled at his zipper and her hand brushed against his erection.

One tug was all it took for her jeans to slip from her hips and drive him to the edge. She wriggled the rest of the way out of them, lowered her panties, and stepped out. He pushed his off and kicked them away along with his briefs, oblivious to where they might have landed. Their bodies melded into one molten combustion of heat.

He slid his hands to her bottom and lifted her up. She wrapped her legs around his waist, and he plunged into her. He could hear her jagged breaths and felt her spasm around him. It was enough to force him over the edge. He drove deep with each eruption, waves of ecstasy slicing through him.

CHAPTER EIGHT

When Jordan awoke the next morning in Reed's bed, the night before all came tumbling back. The storm, the wine, the frantic sex in the dining room, then the slow, solicitous sex after. It all still felt too magnificent to have regrets, and she let the feelings linger. After all, it was just physical.

Had there been no past between them, it would have been easier to believe. She would deal with her heart later if need be and enjoy her freedom while she still had it, she decided as she rolled over. Just as she noticed that Reed was no longer in bed with her, he came strutting into the room carrying a tray with a carafe, two mugs, and a couple of muffins.

"Good morning, beautiful," he said and a smile crossed his lips.

"I was just about to get up and go look for you," she answered and met his smile.

"Well, now there's no need to get out of bed." He set the tray on the nightstand, slid out of his sweat pants, and crawled into bed beside her. "Mm. You smell so good," he muttered as he nuzzled her neck and slid an arm across her.

"And you feel so good," she said as she nestled against him. He was already hard.

He rolled on top of her, settled between her legs, and slid inside her. "I think I should warn you . . . I don't think I will ever be able to get enough of you."

She slid her arms around him, the long, rapturous currents already pulling at her insides. She traced the muscles along his back with her fingertips. "That doesn't sound like such a bad thing."

"I'm glad you see it that way."

He continued with slow, deliberate strokes that sent swells of pleasure rolling through her in the wake of each movement. Their bodies were in perfect sync. There was no awkwardness, no uncertainty that comes with new lovers, only the anticipation of reaching unfathomable heights of euphoria.

When he took her mouth, she closed her eyes. Her thundering heart echoed inside her head as she hung on by a thread. Each thrust hammered away at her control and pushed her closer as her body screamed for that final moment.

The thread snapped and any remnant of control shattered when he said her name and plunged inside her one last time. Every muscle in her body quaked in response, and nothing else mattered in that one glorious moment. She lay there, searching for her next breath, unable to move.

"We're not going to get anything done today if you keep distracting me," he said, skimming his lips over hers.

"I'll just push you away next time," she teased, sliding her fingers down his sides, well aware that would be no easy task.

"You better not," he said, rolling off of her. "Besides, it won't work. I'm afraid nothing short of knocking me unconscious will still the need to have you."

"Let's hope it doesn't have to come to that." She rolled over and propped herself up on an elbow. "Is that coffee over there?"

"It is. Would you like a cup?"

"I would love one."

He filled a mug and handed it to her, then tossed a pillow against the headboard behind her. "Can I interest you in a muffin?"

She scooted back against the pillow. "Would it be one of

Mrs. Doyle's?"

"Of course."

"Then how can I refuse?"

"I don't think you can."

She set her mug on the nightstand beside her, and he handed her a muffin. Then he filled the other cup, pushed a pillow against the headboard behind him, and sat back against it. He took a drink, then set it down and reached for a muffin. "I had an interesting conversation with Gary Carr the other day."

She swallowed a bite of muffin while she pondered the name. "Gary Carr, the congressman?"

"That's the one. Do you have any idea why he's interested in you?"

She lifted her brows, surprised by the question. "I have no idea. I've never met him." She had written a couple of articles on political issues but none about him. "What makes you think he's interested in me?"

"Well." He set down the muffin and picked up his mug. "For starters, he was asking a lot of questions about your case."

"What kind of questions?"

"What evidence the DA has against you? Would I try to make a deal with the DA to protect the details of your relationship with Tanner?" He took a sip of coffee. "Those sort of questions."

"What did you tell him?"

"Nothing."

"Did you ask him why he was interested in my case?" She put down her half-eaten muffin and picked up her coffee.

"Yeah, I did. He said he got caught up in all the media hype about the case."

"Maybe that's all it was." She took a sip of coffee and thought about it. "It seems logical. I am in the headlines, and you know more about my case than anyone."

"I don't think that's all it was. He was too inquisitive. I got the impression he was fishing." He took another sip of coffee, set the mug back down, and tossed the last bite of muffin into his mouth. "Did Tanner ever mention anything about Carr to you?"

"No." She thought about the congressman and knew he was a strait-laced conservative. It's almost too ridiculous a question to ask, she thought, then decided just to ask it. At this point, nobody seemed a likely candidate for murder. "Do you think Congressman Carr has something to do with Steve's death?"

"I don't know."

"Do you know him well enough to know if he is capable of murder?"

"He's a politician, and he's ambitious. Under the right circumstances, that could be a lethal combination." He picked up his mug and emptied it. "I have my investigator digging around for a connection between Carr and Tanner."

He got up and pulled on his sweat pants. "Jordan," he began as he strolled alongside the bed, then stopped at its foot. "Who stands to inherit your assets when you die?"

"What do you mean?"

He turned and peered down at her. "Who has the right to the remainder of the assets you inherited from your parents when you die?"

"What's that got to do with anything?" she asked. She pulled her legs to her chest and folded her arms around them.

"Somebody stands to inherit quite a tidy sum of money if you die. It's—"

"Did you have me investigated?" She cut him off. "How could you?" She tossed her legs over the side of the bed and sprang up. "How dare you?" She grabbed the sheet and pulled it off the bed. Throwing it around herself, she stomped past him, heading for the door. He grabbed her arm and swung her around to face him.

"No." His voice was firm, and his hands were clamped tight around her arms. She knew she wasn't going anywhere. He stared down at her with penetrable eyes. "I did not have you investigated."

"Then how did you know my parents—"

"I was at your parents' funeral," he said, breaking her off. "I wanted to make sure you were . . . taken care of."

"I don't remember seeing you there."

"I didn't want to upset you or give you anything more to deal with. I stayed in the back of the church. After the funeral, when I saw you were surrounded by people who seemed to be able to comfort you, I left."

She lowered her head and struggled to hold back the tears. Everything seemed so overwhelming and the thought of her parents—how unexpectedly and tragically they had died, how much she missed them, and how much she needed them—was too much. "How did you know about my inheritance?"

He loosened his grip. "My father told me." His voice softened. "He's friends with your parents' estate attorney."

She nodded, and there was nothing more she could do about the tears. They spilled down her cheeks. Sorrow, loss, fear, all stabbing at her heart. He slid his arms around her, held her close, and she buried her head in his chest.

"I'm sorry. I promise you, everything will work out," he said, his voice barely above a whisper.

She wiped her tears against the sheet still wrapped around her and drew back. She dropped to the bench at the foot of his bed and steadied herself. "My cousin will inherit everything when I die, but I'm sure she has no idea. I've never told her."

He lowered himself to the bench beside her and tucked an arm around her shoulders. "We can finish talking about this later."

She shook her head. "No. I'm fine. Let's finish."

"Okay." He drew his arm back and stood. He took a few steps and then stopped. "Does anyone else know about your inheritance besides your attorney?"

"I don't think so." She paused for a minute before continuing. "At least not the extent of it. My father and my uncle owned a few properties together, and when my father passed away, he had the title to those properties transferred to my uncle."

"Did your uncle know about your parents' other assets? Did he know how much your parents had left to you?"

"I don't think so. My uncle initially assumed that my father had transferred the title to the properties to him and had transferred the income from the properties to me. My uncle was sending me half the income from those properties and I had to explain to him that he owned the properties completely. I think if he knew the extent of my parents' estate, he would have known I had enough to live on without the income from his properties."

"What did you tell him when you explained that he owned the properties, including the income? Was he curious about what your parents had left you?"

"No. I told him that my parents had left other property to me. He seemed to accept that explanation. I'm sure he assumed that meant that my parents had made sure that I was taken care of financially. He has no idea about my own finances apart from my parents."

He took a few strides before he continued. "Did anyone contest your parents' will?"

"No." She shook her head. "I've never been told that."

"Do you know if your father or parents had any partners or investors other than your uncle?"

"No. I don't know, but I doubt it. They didn't need investors."

"I'd like to talk to your parents' estate attorney."

"Why? I don't understand."

"To rule out the possibility that whoever murdered Tanner may have actually been after you."

"Why would you think that?"

"I don't. I just want to eliminate the possibility."

"All right. I'll call Mr. Braun and tell him to expect to hear from you."

"Good." He reached down and took her hand in his. He pulled her to her feet with a tug and slid his arms around the mountain of sheet wrapped around her. "How would you like to do a little shopping and have dinner out tonight?"

"I like that idea," she replied, surprised. He'd been reluctant to let her go beyond the property's boundaries since they had taken the walk on the beach. She didn't have the vaguest idea why he'd changed his mind, but she wasn't going to question him. "When do we leave?"

"How does an hour sound?"

"It sounds perfect. I'll be ready in an hour," she answered. There was a simple, black, sleeveless shift that had been among the clothes purchased for her. It would be comfortable enough to shop in and perfect for dinner if they didn't go anywhere fancy. "I assume dinner will be casual?"

"Your preference."

"Then it's casual."

An hour later they were zipping east on Montauk Highway with the top down on Reed's *Porsche*, the humid September air whipping through their hair, and Mick Jagger's voice belting out a song from the speakers.

She glanced over and saw Reed check his rear-view mirror for the fifth time since they'd turned on Montauk. "What is it?" she asked.

"The same sedan has been following us for the last few miles, and I can't shake the feeling that it isn't just a coincidence. New York plates. That's all I can make out. The sun visor obscures the driver's face, so I can't tell if it's a man or a woman." He released a slow breath. "Between the person on the beach and the one now following us, it sure seems like someone is keeping an eye on you." He glanced over at her. "Let's get rid of whoever it is, shall we?"

He stomped on the clutch and threw the shifter into a higher gear. When he released the clutch and punched down on the gas, the car shot down the road like an arrow from a bow. In seconds, the sedan was nothing more than a speck on the horizon.

"There's only one thing I can think of right now that's better than this," he shouted over the music.

"What would that be?" She had long since given up trying to keep her hair tied back. To no avail, she tucked a handful behind her ear, which immediately flew loose.

He looked over and flicked an eyebrow. When she rolled her eyes, the corners of his lips curved upwards.

She braced herself as he shifted into a lower gear and swerved onto Daniels Hole Road. A mile further, he pulled into the East Hampton Airport.

"What are we doing here?" she asked as the roadster came to a halt in a parking space.

"We're going shopping and to dinner," he replied, hopping out and circling around to the passenger side. He pulled open her door and offered his hand.

She took it and stepped from the car. "Here?"

"Not exactly. We're going to a quiet little town in the Hudson Valley." He tossed the door closed and glimpsed back at the road. "You probably won't be recognized there, and if you are, by the time the press or anyone else finds out, we'll be back here. At least, that's what I'm counting on."

"Isn't this a little extreme for shopping and dinner?"

"Under the circumstances, no." He slid his arm around her waist, and they strolled toward the terminal. "It serves another purpose, too. I had my secretary make reservations at several inns and bed and breakfasts under names with just enough similarities to ours to keep the paparazzi busy for a few days. If you are recognized, this will keep them away from your apartment while we try to find out what the person who left the scarf was looking for."

"When are we going back to the city?"

"Tomorrow." He pushed open the door to the terminal and led her inside. "But forget about tomorrow, and let's enjoy today. I see my pilot. Let's board."

Chapter Nine

Hoping to be less conspicuous in a taxi, Reed had a cab pick him and Jordan up to take them to her apartment. Traffic wasn't as heavy on a Sunday, and it didn't take long to get there. It was an older building, Reed observed when she pointed it out to the driver, and it still held the original charm of the neighborhood. There wasn't a reporter or a cameraman in sight when they pulled to the curb. He assumed his plan was working and that the paparazzi were roaming around the Hudson Valley searching for her.

"It's nice to see you again, Miss Maxwell," the doorman said when they climbed from the cab. He ushered them inside. Reed took a step ahead of Jordan to shield her when a young man strode toward them. The man smiled at Jordan, then nodded at Reed.

"Reed, this is Ernesto," she said, and the man extended his hand to Reed.

"It's nice to meet you, sir," Ernesto said. "I will do whatever I can to help Miss Maxwell. You just let me know what I can do."

"Thank you, Ernesto," Reed replied, shaking his hand and guessing, from his moderate accent, that he was from Puerto Rico. "It's a pleasure to meet you, as well. Would you mind coming up to Miss Maxwell's apartment with us?"

"No, sir. Of course, I will come." He turned and headed for the elevator. The doors slid apart when he pushed the button. He put an arm across one of the doors and waited for Jordan and Reed to enter. He then followed them inside and pushed the button for the top floor.

"How is your son doing, Ernesto?" Jordan asked with a warm smile. "Is he finished with the chemotherapy?"

"Yes. Very good," he replied with a nod. "The doctors say he is doing very good, and I can see. He doesn't look so sick anymore."

"I'm glad. And your wife? Is she well?"

"Yes." He nodded again. "She is relieved. She is finally able to sleep again."

"Good. And what about you? How are you doing?"

"I'm good." He shook his head and glanced at the floor. "It was a hard thing, but I'm good. And thank you for asking." When the doors slid open, he again put an arm across one of the doors. "After you, please," he said, then followed them to her apartment.

Reed stepped in front of Jordan and took her key from her. "I'll open it," he said and slid the key into the lock. When he pushed the door open, he led them into the foyer.

He glanced around as he and Ernesto followed her through the foyer. It was clear that the interior had been gutted and redone. He guessed her apartment was originally two separate units, and he wondered how much of a hand, if any, she'd had in the renovation. Everything was high-end and exquisitely feminine, from the sheer drapes to the luxurious velvet mauve sofa. "Please, have a seat, won't you?" she asked, gesturing toward the sofa.

"Thank you," Ernesto said with a curt nod and sat down on the sofa's edge. He clasped his hands and settled them in his lap.

Reed lowered himself to a white tufted chair across from Ernesto and assumed that Ben had found the scarf near the gold-trimmed coffee table that separated them. He glanced around to see if anything else might have been left behind. Seeing nothing, he turned to Ernesto.

"May I get either of you anything to drink?" Jordan offered. "A glass of water, soda?"

"No, thank you," Ernesto replied.

"I'm fine, Jordan. Thanks," Reed replied. "Thank you for coming in a little earlier for your shift, Ernesto. I appreciate it."

"You're welcome. I am happy to do anything I can. I saw on the television what is wrong."

"You phrased that correctly. It is wrong, and I'm going to right it. Now, I'm going to test your memory. I need you to think back over the last couple of months."

"Yes, sir." He nodded. "I can do that."

"Good. Then tell me if you can recall at any time over the last couple of months if anyone ever asked you to let them into Ms. Maxwell's apartment."

"Oh, no, no," he said, rocking back and then forward again. "I never do that. I never let anyone into an apartment unless I am told by the owner." He glanced at Jordan and then shifted his gaze back to Reed. "Miss Maxwell never told me to do that and I never did that. No."

"I'm glad to hear you never did that, Ernesto, but did anyone ever ask you to let them into her apartment?"

"No." He shook his head. "No one asked me that. I would remember."

"Do you remember if Jordan ever had any visitors while she was gone?"

"Yes. Her friend, Charles, came a few times when she was not here."

"Did he go up to her apartment any of those times?"

"No, he did not go up. He just asked me if she was home. Then he would leave when I told him she wasn't home. Except for one time, he went up when I told him she was not home. But she was home that time, and he told me she was waiting for him."

"Was that a couple of weeks ago, Ernesto?" Jordan asked. "When I was wearing the wig?"

"Yes, ma'am. It was that time."

Reed glanced at her, then slid his gaze back to Ernesto. "Why did you tell him that Ms. Maxwell wasn't home if she was?"

"I'm sorry." He looked at Jordan as he answered, his voice thick with regret. "I thought you didn't want anyone to know you were home because, you know, you were wearing a disguise, and the newsmen were all around asking me to let them know when you came home. I'm sorry I lied. I did it to protect you."

"No, Ernesto," she quickly reassured him. "You did the right thing. I knew you would lie for me, and that's why I thought it was all right to come home. You did what I expected you to do."

"Yes," Reed agreed, "you did the right thing. I wasn't implying that you didn't."

"Okay, good," Ernesto said. "I never want to do anything that will hurt Miss Maxwell." He turned to her. "That was why I acted like I didn't know you. I didn't mean to be rude."

"I knew that, and you did a good job."

Reed pulled the scarf from his briefcase and set it on the coffee table. He had placed it in a transparent, plastic bag to protect the integrity of any DNA or other evidence that might be on it. "Ernesto, have you ever seen anyone come into the building wearing this scarf?"

He studied it for a moment before he spoke. "No. I don't think so, but I ignore clothes. Unless it's something silly, then, of course, I notice. But there is nothing silly about that scarf. I pay attention to the faces. I watch the faces that come in and go out."

"Is it possible for anyone to access the apartment keys?"

"No, sir. They are kept in a locked box, in a locked drawer, in a locked room. They are not touched. They are for emergencies only. And there is a procedure to get a key. A paper must be filled out, and permission has to be received."

"What if someone came and said they had a surprise gift that they wanted to leave inside an apartment? Would they be allowed to do that?"

"No, sir. That is not an emergency. If they want to leave a gift, we would take it and put it in the office. The concierge would take care of it from there."

"All right, Ernesto," he said, rising. "Thank you for your time. I may call you if I have any more questions."

"Yes." Ernesto stood and straightened his jacket.

Jordan pushed herself up and took Ernesto's arm as she escorted him back to the door. "You'll give that little boy of yours a kiss for me, won't you, Ernesto?"

"Yes, of course. I give him lots of kisses, and I'll give him one for you."

Reed extended his hand to Ernesto as he opened the door. "It was nice to meet you, Ernesto."

"Thank you." He shook his hand, turned to leave, and then stopped. "Oh, I should send Clive up?"

"Yes, please."

"Okay," he said and started down the hallway.

Reed examined the door for a moment, then satisfied that there appeared to be no evidence of forced entry, closed it. "It looks like whoever left that scarf entered your apartment with a key."

"You heard Ernesto," she said as she started toward the kitchen. "The emergency keys are locked away."

"What about the key you keep in the light fixture. Who knows about that key?"

She stopped and turned back to him. "How —" she began, then caught herself. "Ben?"

He grinned. "I told you. He reports to me."

She turned again and walked into the kitchen. "I'm beginning to feel like Ben is more of a spy than a bodyguard."

"He's looking out for you." He sat on one of the stools at the counter, surveying the kitchen. The cabinets were nicely done, and the appliances were top of the line. He wondered how much time she spent in the kitchen. The countertops were bare, and everything was spotless. "It's his job."

She opened the refrigerator and frowned. "Would you like a bottle of water?" she asked, pulling one out for herself.

"Yeah, I'll take one."

She tossed him the one in her hand and pulled out another for herself. "Remind me to throw out the trash before we leave," she said, closing the door.

He cocked a brow. "Is something growing in there?"

"More like dying, and I'm afraid it might mutate into something unrecognizable if I forget to throw it out."

"Where are your trash bags?" he asked, getting up and rounding the counter.

"Under here." She pulled a small, white plastic bag out from under the counter and handed it to him.

"I take it you don't generate much trash," he remarked, snapping open the bag.

"Not too much." She leaned against the counter and watched him.

"You don't eat much, either," he commented when he opened the refrigerator. The few apples she had left were now round little wrinkles of rot. The cheese was moldy, and the ham was green.

"I haven't exactly been here."

"Even so, I'm betting you don't cook much." He pulled the rotted items out, dropped them into the bag, twisted the top, and tied it into a knot. "Is there anything else you need to throw out?"

"I'm sure there isn't. We can toss that on our way out. The

trash chute is next to the elevator."

"I can take it now," he said, setting the bag on the counter beside her and sliding his arms around her waist. "That is unless you have something else in mind." He brushed his lips over hers and slid them down her neck. His hands glided up her back under her shirt.

"Aren't we expecting a visitor?"

A knock at the door interrupted them, and he pulled back. "That must be Clive. His timing is impeccable." He grabbed the bag to put it outside the door and headed toward the foyer.

She followed him from the kitchen.

Reed pulled the door open, and Charles stepped into the foyer. He gave a curt nod to Reed as he passed him and strode toward Jordan. He gave her a hug as he spoke. "It's so good to see that you're finally home. It seems things have quieted down about the case. How are you doing?"

She returned the hug, then pulled back. "I'm doing fine, Charles. How are things at the bookstore?"

"Everybody's asking about you."

"Excuse me, buddy," Reed interrupted. "Would you mind telling me how you knew Jordan was here?"

Charles turned and looked up at him. "I was walking past the corner to get a sandwich and saw you two get out of the taxi."

"So you thought you would just invite yourself up?"

"Reed, Charles is a friend of mine," she said before turning back to Charles. "But you should call before you come up, Charles."

"Yeah, Charles, friends don't intrude," Reed said, ignoring the smugness in his eyes. "They call first."

"I'm sorry," he answered, then turned to Jordan. "I guess I should have called. I'm sure you're busy trying to get settled back in."

Jordan looked past Reed when the elevator dinged, and Reed turned and watched Clive step into the hallway. "Actually, Charles, now isn't a good time to visit. Reed and I are working."

"Oh." He adjusted his glasses and cleared his throat. "I . . . I wasn't intending to stay. I have to get back to the bookstore."

"Well, thank you for stopping by. It was good to see you again, even if only for a moment."

"Should I come back, sir?" Clive asked Reed as he approached the apartment.

"No, please come in." Reed stepped aside to let Clive pass. He placed his free hand on Charles's shoulder and turned him toward the door. "Another time, perhaps, Charles. And on your way out, why don't you take care of this for Jordan," he added, shoving the trash bag against his chest and pushing him into the hallway. He tossed the door shut behind him.

Jordan greeted Clive and took a box as he handed it to her. When she glanced at the contents, Reed noticed her twitch.

"Clive, we haven't met," Reed said, extending his hand. "Reed Carrington."

He took his hand. "It's nice to meet you, Mr. Carrington."

"Thank you, and how are you today, Clive?"

"Fine, sir."

"Good. What did you bring with you?" he asked, dropping his gaze to the box that Jordan was holding. It appeared to be full of mail in different sizes of envelopes. He noticed one addressed to *Bitch Maxwell,* another to *Murderer.*

"Mail, sir." He turned to Jordan and frowned. "I'm sorry, miss."

"Don't worry about it, Clive." She forced a smile. "Let's have a seat in the living room, shall we?"

Reed took the box and set it on the table in the foyer. He'd have someone go through it later to determine whether there were any threats to be concerned about or in case there was something in there from the murderer. In any event, he didn't want Jordan going through that box of horror.

The interview went much the same as the one with Ernesto, as did the one after that with the concierge. Nowhere. No leads. No clues.

"We're not making very good progress," Jordan remarked after the concierge had left. She walked back to the kitchen and dropped to one of the stools at the counter. She took a sip from the bottle of water she had left there.

Reed could hear the disappointment in her voice. It was colored with frustration. He strolled up behind her, slid his hands on her shoulders, and gave them a soft squeeze. He worked his hands over her shoulders and neck. Her muscles were tight, as hard as granite. "We're not done here yet. We have to see if we can find what whoever owns the scarf was looking for."

"I know." She lowered her head, letting it hang. "That feels good." He leaned down, brushed her hair aside with his chin, and then grazed her neck with his lips, leaving a trail of soft, little kisses.

"This is nothing compared to what I'll do to you later."

"Mm. I can't wait," she muttered.

"Neither can I," he whispered and drew back. "So let's finish what we have to do here. Do you have any disposable gloves?"

"Yes. I have a box of latex gloves. What do you want those for?"

"So we don't leave any more prints. I'm going to have the police dust any areas you find that have been disturbed."

She slid from the chair and walked over to the sink. Bending down, she pulled a couple pairs of gloves from a box, then returned to Reed. "Here's a pair for you," she said, handing him a pair.

"Thanks," he said, struggling to pull them on. "Where do

you want to start?"

She released a long breath. "The office. I know she was in there."

He followed her to her office. It was dark, and with the curtains closed, it was noticeably cooler than the rest of her apartment. "It's like a cave in here. I hope you don't spend much time in here."

"I spend most of my time in here. It's conducive to writing." She glanced around. "I'm not sure where to start or what to look for."

She reached for the light switch, and he grabbed her hand. "I don't think we want to let anyone else know you're here. Just in case."

"My drapes are lined with black-out fabric. No one can see in any better than we can see out." When he released her hand, she flipped the switch, and light flooded the room. "Besides, you saw it out there, and you heard Charles. Things have quieted down. In fact, I was thinking about staying here now."

"Yeah, things may have quieted down, but that's temporary. The photographers scouting the Hudson Valley looking for you will probably be back when they figure out you're no longer there."

"Well, they don't know I'm here." She pulled her desk chair out, spun it around, and sat down. "As long as I have groceries delivered, I can be holed up inside for weeks or longer."

"You can forget about staying here." He sat down on the edge of a chair near a wall of bookshelves primarily full of books. "That's not going to happen. We still don't know if whoever killed Tanner was after you. Besides, I saw the mail you're getting. If someone's looking to avenge Tanner's death, they'll be watching your apartment."

He saw the frown before she swiveled her chair and

opened a desk drawer. "I guess I'm not safe here yet. And I won't be even if I'm acquitted. Unless people know who killed Steve, there will always be people who think I did, and one of them could want to kill me."

"Let's focus on what we have to do here." He got up and moved across the room to the closet. "Keep going through those drawers. And what about the top of your desk. Is anything out of place? Missing?" He opened one of the doors and peered inside. More books.

"Nothing so far." She closed a drawer and opened another one.

"Boot up your computer. See if any of your files have been tampered with."

"Okay." She tapped the button on the surge protector, then went back to the drawers while the computer hummed and clicked.

"Are you sure Ben found the scarf in your living room?"

"Yes, that's what he said. On the floor by the coffee table."

"There's not much in your living room in terms of storage. Why would someone bother going in there when everything in there can be seen from the foyer?" He thought for a moment as he paced a few steps. "It doesn't make sense."

"It doesn't make sense that anyone was in my apartment at all." She shut the last drawer to her desk. "Nothing. Nothing's missing."

"Take a look at your shelves. Does anything appear out of order? Missing?"

She got up and took a few steps along the length of the wall, scrutinizing each shelf. She took a few more steps and ran her finger along a shelf, leaving a trail in the dust. She stopped and smiled at a photograph. "My mother told me this was our first family portrait. I was two years old." She chuckled. "She said she had to keep giving me candies to suck on to keep me still."

He strolled up behind her and studied the photograph. "You look like a little angel in that frilly dress."

"I was a terrible two. I doubt I was an angel at that stage of my life." She took a few more strides and continued looking over the shelves.

He took a step nearer to the shelf for a closer look. "Did you drag your finger along this shelf?" he asked, noticing the line in the dust.

"Yes, and I know my shelves are dusty. My maid only comes when I'm here, and I haven't been here, remember?"

"Did you move the picture?"

"No, I didn't touch the picture." She turned and looked at him. "Why?"

"The dust is disturbed around the picture. Someone picked up the picture, then put it back down, but not in the exact same place."

"Let me see," she said, taking the few steps back.

"Here," he said, pointing to the left corner of the frame. "You can tell it was placed back about an inch to the right and a little further back on the shelf."

"Yes." She studied the surface of the shelf. "I see what you mean. Why would someone take the time to study a photograph?"

"I don't know," he replied with a shrug. "But that's a good question."

"My computer's booted up," she said, glancing at her computer. She hurried over, dropped down to her chair, and swiveled it around.

"Let's start with your writing," he said, walking over. "See if any files containing anything you've written have been opened since you used your computer last."

"Okay." She clicked open file explorer, clicked on a few folders, and then studied her files. "I haven't used this computer since I started staying at Steve's." She continued scrolling down her files as she talked. "I did everything on my laptop. It doesn't look like anything I've written has been opened since I closed it last."

"Check your e-mails. Can any of your email accounts be accessed only from this computer, or can you access all your accounts from your laptop?"

"I have an email address I use for just junk. I don't bother to check it from my laptop." She opened the e-mail account and clicked on the inbox. "It looks like none of the last e-mails I received over the past two months have been opened. If someone was on my computer, they weren't interested in my e-mails, either."

"Okay, check whatever other programs you have on your computer, and see if you can determine if anyone dug around in them. Maybe someone was interested in your finances. Check any banking or stock programs you might have."

She continued clicking and scrolling while he looked for more signs of a disturbance on the bookshelves. "If the woman in my apartment turned on my computer, she didn't open any of my programs," she said after a few minutes.

"Well, she seemed curious about your photographs," he remarked, studying another picture. "There are a few more that were moved, too." He turned back around to her. "Let's see if we can find anything interesting in the other rooms."

"Okay." She nodded and led him down the hall.

"What's in this room?" he asked, tapping his knuckles on a closed door a few feet down from Jordan's office.

"Just boxes," she answered, reaching for the doorknob. She pushed open the door and stepped inside. A dozen or so plain, brown boxes were stacked in a corner. "They are some things I packed from my parents' house. I haven't had a chance to go through them."

"What sort of things?" He meandered over to the boxes,

bent over, and examined a few. "You didn't label them?"

"No." She walked over to him, brushed her fingers over a box, let them linger. "They're personal things. Photo albums, a journal my mother kept for me, a stuffed clown my father bought for me. Things that wouldn't mean much to anyone else."

"They've been taped over," he said, lifting one and studying the one beneath it. "And very neatly. Did you re-tape them?"

"No." She leaned down and inspected a box. The original tape had been very neatly sliced at the edges of the box and a piece of tape reapplied over it, perfectly aligned. "Are they all like this?"

"It looks like it," he said, looking over the last box.

"Why would someone go through all of them? Wouldn't you think after opening the first few boxes and seeing what's inside, they would lose interest?"

"Maybe, unless they were looking for something in particular and weren't finding it. Or maybe they were looking for something belonging to your parents."

"But what would that have to do with Steve?" She dropped down onto one of the boxes. "None of this makes any sense. It seems that the more we discover, the more confusing things seem."

"It's just like a puzzle. It'll make sense when we get all of the pieces in order." He reached for her hand and pulled her up to him. "At least we're finding the pieces."

She nodded. "I just hope we can find them all."

"We won't stop looking until we do."

CHAPTER TEN

They woke up early the next morning at Reed's apartment in the city.

"Are you sure you don't want me to have something delivered?" he asked as he adjusted his tie. He glanced at her reflection behind him in the mirror. His robe, miles too big, was cinched loosely at her waist.

The corner of his mouth turned up as he thought about what was hidden beneath it. Soft, pale flesh. Luscious curves. It would take one quick yank to have that robe at her feet. He could feel the knot tightening in his gut just thinking about it.

"I'm sure."

He turned and took the few strides to her. He tugged at the belt of the robe until it fell loose. The front of his robe parted, revealing a teasing amount of flesh, enough to twist the knot.

She arched a brow. "Don't you have to go to work?"

"I'm the boss." He slid his hands under the front of the robe and lifted it from her shoulders. "I work when I want to." He let the robe fall to the floor.

She stood, naked, while he unfastened his belt, unhooked his trousers, and slid them off. He laid them over the back of a chair. When he lifted his hands to his tie, she pushed them away and wrapped her fingers around it. She drew him toward her as she stepped backward toward the bed.

She lowered herself onto the bed and pulled him down to her. He settled between her legs. He knew she was ready, but he lingered outside of her. He wanted to tease her. He wanted to make sure that she wanted him as much as he wanted her.

He dragged his lips between her breasts, leaving a trail of kisses. He let his fingers glide down her side, along her hip, and heard her breath catch when he reached the inside of her thigh.

She tugged on his tie, still wrapped around her fist, and brought him back to her mouth. He kissed her deeply and entered her part way. He withdrew when she arched her back, and a desperate moan escaped her lips. It fueled the passion racing through his veins.

He entered her again. She released his tie and slid her hands under his shirt. As her fingers traveled down his back, tiny strands of lust tugged at the knot in his gut, and he knew he could no longer hold back. He pounded into her, and she took each assault with a gasp of pleasure. The knot snapped when she called out his name, and an explosion ripped through him. He peeled himself off and collapsed next to her.

"You make it very difficult to get out the door," he managed as he pulled his tie loose and unfastened the top button of his shirt.

"You don't make it very easy to let you leave."

"I'm glad to hear that," he said, pushing aside the nagging prick to his conscience that had developed over the past couple of weeks. He reached for her hand and lifted it to his lips. He planted a soft kiss across her fingers before releasing it, then swung his legs over the side of the bed and sat up.

Within half an hour, he had showered, dressed again, and left. Jordan had two hours before Ben would be there to pick her up and take her to Reed's office to meet with the investigator. She decided to watch the morning news before showering, hoping she wouldn't be a part of it. She found the remote control on the nightstand and pressed the power button. The screen on the television remained blank. She aimed the remote control and tried it a few more times before looking for batteries.

She wandered into Reed's office and looked around. It was as tastefully decorated as the rest of his apartment, and as with the rest of his apartment, nothing less than what she would expect in the Upper East Side. Burgundy and navy striped curtains with a hint of gold running through framed a window that offered a view of Central Park.

She looked down at the people milling around in the park for a brief minute before strolling over to the desk. She ran a finger along the rich, lustrous mahogany wood and then sat down. The drawers would be neat and organized, if the top of his desk was any indication. It was a far cry from her desk, but she knew where everything was, and her spare batteries were in the bottom drawer. She leaned down and pulled open the bottom drawer, gambling that maybe he kept them in the same place. The drawer was lined with files, each marked. Her gaze caught a familiar name. Curious, she lifted the file to see if it was the same person she had known. There was a report in the file from an investigator complete with photographs of her and Craig Wagner, the name on the file. The report also listed every date they'd had for the few weeks they had gone out. When she saw the processed check for $10,000 payable to Craig, dated just after their last date, she went numb.

She snatched another file out of the drawer. There was another report, other pictures, another check. She grabbed another file. It was a file on Steve Tanner. Stunned, she fell back against the chair, staring at the scattered contents of the files on his desk. She felt as if she'd been delivered a dagger to the heart.

Her mind raced for answers, and she wondered what Reed had done and why he'd paid the men she had dated. Her mind reeled from the shock of it, and she wondered if he had killed Steve because he couldn't pay him off. That' ridiculous, she told herself, trying to make some sense of it. Reed was defending her. He wouldn't be defending her if he wanted to hurt her. *Unless he loses the trial.* She shook the thought from her mind. It was ludicrous. Reed wasn't a murderer. Yet, it didn't make sense. But nothing she knew made any sense.

She needed to think. She needed to get away. She snapped up the receiver and punched in the number for *Between the Pages*.

"Hello, darling," Blair sang out as she waltzed through the door of Reed's office.

"You seem in rather high spirits today, Blair." He pushed himself up from his chair and stood to greet her.

"Don't get up," she said, too late, waving her hand. She planted a kiss on his cheek, then wiped away the smudge of lipstick she had left with her finger.

"You're looking lovely today. Lunch plans?"

"Of course." She adjusted the top of her *Dior* suit as she strutted over to the window and glanced out over the skyline. "There's always something or other going on."

"So, to what do I owe the pleasure of this visit?" He was pretty sure he knew. There had been another article about Jordan in the morning paper, and he was betting his mother had read it.

"Please, I don't need a reason to stop in on my son." She turned toward him. "So, how is work going?"

"Are you asking in general or about Jordan's case?"

"In general, but now that you mention it, how is her case coming along?" She sauntered over to the wet bar, lifted a glass, examined it. "Good, I hope."

"Since when do you care how Jordan's doing?" He got up,

crossed to a credenza, and poured a cup of coffee. "Would you like a cup?" he offered.

"No, thank you." She set the glass down. "I didn't ask about her. I asked about her case. It's getting quite a bit of publicity. It seems to be what everyone is talking about."

"Would those conversations have anything to do with the article in the paper this morning?" He took a sip of coffee, then strolled back to his desk.

"You know I don't read the paper, but I did hear she inherited a boatload of money." She wandered back in the direction of his desk. "Money fascinates people. For some reason, people pay more attention to things when they happen to someone with money."

"This case has been getting a lot of attention because of Steve Tanner. I don't think it's going to get any more attention just because now everyone knows Jordan inherited some money. And, since when are you concerned about my getting too much publicity?"

"Well, I heard that her fingerprints were on the knife that killed that musician and that she was covered in his blood when the police found her. How in the world are you ever going to win a case against that kind of evidence?" She stopped at one of the client chairs facing his desk and rested her arms across the top of it.

"I see." He took another sip of coffee. "So, you're worried about my embarrassing you should I lose the trial?"

"Not me, darling." She shrugged. "I can accept that sometimes you win, sometimes you lose. I'm just concerned about what a loss might do to your reputation."

"You needn't lose any sleep over that, Blair. I don't plan on losing."

"For your sake, I hope you win. Oh, my," she continued, wrinkling a brow. "Don't tell me the Carr boy is in trouble again."

"What are you talking about?"

"The scarf," she said, rounding the chair and lifting the plastic bag from the corner of his desk. "This is Victoria Carr's scarf. Has she been in to see you about her son again?"

"What makes you think that's Victoria's?"

"I should know, darling. I picked it out for her. It was a gift to thank her for organizing a luncheon to honor someone or other." She turned it over in her hands and opened a corner of the bag. "Mmm. Yes, that's her perfume. Giorgio. It smells divine."

"Excuse me, Mr. Carrington. I'm sorry to interrupt," Rose said over the intercom.

"Yes, Rose."

"Mr. Connor is here, sir."

"Tell him I'll be with him in a moment." His mouth lifted into a smile as he rose from the chair and circled his desk. "Blair, I can't tell you how glad I am that you stopped by," he said, sliding an arm around her shoulder as he took the bag and accompanied her to the door.

"I'm so glad. Perhaps, I should stop by more often?"

"Perhaps."

"Good. Goodbye, darling."

Harry Connor strutted into the office as soon as Blair cleared the doorway. "How are you, Reed?" he asked, offering his hand.

"Not so bad, Harry, and you?" He took his hand and shook it. "Come in, have a seat," he said, closing the door.

"Thank you." Harry looked around at the empty office. "Ms. Maxwell's not here yet?"

"You're a little early," Reed answered, glancing at his watch. "But she should be here shortly. Last I spoke with her, she was planning on being here."

"Actually, I wanted to talk to you before she got here."

"All right. Sit," he said, motioning to the client chairs facing his desk. "We can chat at my desk. Can I get you some coffee?"

"No, thanks. I'm good." He strode over to the client chairs and sat down.

"What's on your mind, Harry?" he asked, lowering himself to his chair.

"I dug up some exciting information." He pulled out a pair of reading glasses from his pocket, slipped them on, and flipped over a few pages on his pad. "I think we got ourselves a real good suspect."

Chapter Eleven

"I'm so glad you could get away from the store to drive me, Charles," Jordan said as she tossed her bag onto the backseat. "I feel like I just need to be by myself for a few days to clear my head and rethink everything that's happened."

"I'm happy to do it. I picked us up a couple of coffees," he said, handing her a cup.

"Thank you. That was thoughtful." She took the cup, took a sip, and then secured her seat belt.

"You're welcome." He tossed her a smile and eased into traffic. "You know you can count on me. I'd do anything for you, Jordan."

"I know. You're a good friend." She rested her head against the headrest and released a long sigh. "I'm sorry I haven't had much time for you the last couple of months. My life's been so crazy."

"I know. It sure has. Don't worry about it."

"Mm. This tastes good," she said, taking another sip.

"It's just how you like it, a little cream, one sugar."

She glanced over at him, felt a hint of uneasiness, then dismissed it. "Right."

"So what happened in your case?"

"What do you mean?"

"You know, what happened to make you want to be alone, rethink, clear your head?"

She sipped her coffee while she thought and then decided not to tell him about the files. "No one thing. The stress of being charged with murder and the lack of progress in finding the real killer is getting to me."

"So, your high-falutin attorney doesn't have a clue or any leads on who may have killed Turner?"

"Not yet." When he turned at the next street, she glanced out the window. "Why are we going west? Shouldn't we be going north?" She had called a quaint, little inn she'd seen in the small town in the Hudson Valley the weekend she'd been there with Reed. They had vacancies and she'd made a reservation. She was counting on the press not going up there even if she was recognized, not having found her there the last time she was there.

"Eventually. I'm trying to avoid traffic. Save us some time."

"Oh. Good idea." She took the last sip of coffee and lowered the empty cup to the floor.

"Did you read the paper this morning?" he asked.

"No. I was going to watch the news, but I couldn't get the remote to work and the television was too high to reach." Feeling tired, she blinked and tried to focus. Why?"

"I didn't read it, either." She saw him glance over at her. "Are you all right?"

"Yes, I'm . . . I'm just tired all of a sudden." It was getting hard to think. She let her head fall against the headrest. "I would think the coffee would have perked me up. I guess the stress of everything is taking its toll. Do you mind if I recline the seat a little?"

"Not at all. In fact, why don't you close your eyes, get some rest."

"You don't mind?" It was getting impossible to keep her eyes open. "I won't be very good company if I'm sleeping," she said, her words slurring just before her eyes closed and her head fell to one side.

"Our suspect doesn't happen to be Congressman Gary Carr, does it?" Reed asked. How ironic it is that Blair is the one to solve the mystery about the scarf, he thought, remembering his father's words. Now, they needed to find out just what the congressman and his wife had to do with Steve Tanner.

"No, it's not the congressman," Harry answered. "Why? Did you find out something about him?"

"I did, but who are you talking about?"

"That Charles Olgalvie fellow you had me check out. The one you said owned the bookstore?"

"What about him?" Reed set his elbows on the chair and leaned back. He hadn't liked the little twerp from the beginning.

"Well, for starters, he doesn't own the bookstore, at least not *Between the Pages*. He's just an employee there. Some fellow by the name of Herman Crane owns it."

"So, the guy's a liar. What else do you have on him?"

"He's got a very interesting criminal record. Seems he likes to stalk women. He's had six restraining orders filed against him. Three by one woman, two by another, and one by the boyfriend of the woman who took out the two restraining orders. The last one was as recent as two years ago."

"That's interesting. Have you talked to the women or the boyfriend?"

"Not yet, but I have someone on it." He pulled off his glasses and set them on the desk. "It gets better. According to three police reports, he physically threatened his two female victims and actually attacked the male victim."

"How did he attack him?"

"That's the clincher. His weapon of choice is a knife. The same kind that was found in Tanner. A Buck drop point hunting knife."

Reed shot forward so quickly his chair leveled with a clank.

"I think you have something there, Harry."

"Yeah, you see why I didn't want to tell you in front of your client. This Olgalvie fellow is a friend of hers, right?"

He nodded. "Good call." He didn't need Jordan letting their suspicions slip to the little shit, intentionally or inadvertently.

"It's possible he got tired of being just a friend. You know what I mean?"

"I sure do."

"Do you think this is enough to get the DA to dismiss the charges against your client?"

He shook his head. "No." It was good information, but all circumstantial, especially compared to what the DA thought he had on Jordan. "And I don't want to blow our chances of proving this sleaze bag is the killer by doing anything prematurely."

"So, what are you going to do?"

"I'm going to set a trap for the son-of-a-bitch," he said, wondering if Charles had been the one on the beach in Water Mill and in the car behind them on the way to the airport and wondering whether he'd already unknowingly set a trap. "And I'll be the bait."

"Sounds dangerous," Harry said, shaking his head. "And it sounds like you're gonna need me."

"All right." He glanced at his watch. "We'll finish talking about this after Jordan leaves. She should be here any minute."

Harry nodded. "What did you find out about Carr?"

"That scarf," he said, nodding toward the edge of his desk, "belongs to his wife. Somehow it ended up in Jordan's apartment."

"Hmm." Harry paused for a moment. "I can't imagine what the connection is between Carr's wife and Olgalvie."

"Maybe there isn't one." He settled back in his chair. "But

if there is one, we'll find it. What else have you got to report?"

Harry reached up and retrieved his glasses. He slid them on and then glanced down at his pad. "The actress that had the boy with Tanner. Seems the split-up wasn't real amicable. She blamed Tanner for everything wrong in her life, including her stalled career."

Reed lifted his hand. "Let's save that for Jordan. And everything else you got." He glanced at his watch again. She was late. He tapped the button on his intercom.

"Yes, Mr. Carrington?" The voice of Rose's assistant spilled from the intercom.

"Have there been any calls for me?"

"Yes, sir. Ben Clausen called for you about fifteen minutes ago."

An uneasy feeling pricked at his gut, and he bounced forward in his chair. "You should have put him through. Why didn't you put him through?"

"I . . . I'm sorry, sir," the girl stammered. "You were in a meeting. Rose didn't tell me I could interrupt you."

"Get him on the phone immediately," he ordered.

"Yes, sir."

"Maybe he called to tell you they're running late," Harry suggested.

Before he could answer, the assistant was back on the intercom. "Mr. Clausen is on line one, Mr. Carrington. He just called back."

He punched the button and grabbed the receiver. "Where are you, Ben?"

"I'm still at your apartment, sir."

"Is Jordan with you?"

"No. The door was unlocked, so I came inside when she didn't answer. She wasn't here, but I figured she would be back since she's expecting me, and I'm still waiting. I hope that's okay."

"It's fine." The prick turned into a gnawing bite as he asked the following question. "Are there any signs of a struggle in my apartment?" From the corner of his eye, he saw Harry slide to the edge of his chair.

"No. I'm sorry, I looked around your apartment to make sure Jordan hadn't fallen or was lying unconscious somewhere. The only thing I saw that may be out of order are some files strewn across the desk in the office, and the bottom drawer was left open. Oh, and it's possible someone may have used the phone on the desk. The receiver wasn't seated all the way in the cradle."

"Shit," he muttered under his breath. It never occurred to him that Jordan might find the files. The last thing he needed was to lose Jordan's trust. "All right. Listen, I want you to check the caller ID on the phone. See where the last few calls were made to. Then check with the concierge and see if anyone saw Jordan leave. If so, find out when and who she left with."

"Yes, sir."

"Then come down here to my office."

"I'm on it."

Reed tossed down the receiver, and Harry asked, "What do you want me to do?"

"Wait here until you hear from me." He shoved his chair back and shot up to his feet.

"Where are you going?"

"To Jordan's apartment," he called over his shoulder. "Get the car around front, now," he ordered as he snatched his suit coat from the closet and hurried past Rose's assistant.

The ride to Jordan's apartment seemed like an eternity and he cursed himself the entire trip. He could kick himself for forgetting about those files. How could he have been so careless? The prick of guilt was now a full-blown gnaw of re-morse, and the fact that he'd fallen in love with her hit hard. There was no way he could lose her again.

As they rounded the corner of her street, he saw a parked car with someone sitting inside. A photographer, he assumed. It wasn't a good sign. It meant that she probably wasn't there. "Wait here," he told his driver as he shoved open the door and sprang from the car. He was glad to see Ernesto on duty. "Is Jordan here?"

"No, sir. I haven't seen her."

"Ernesto, it's important that you not cover for her."

"I understand," he said with a nod.

"Her life could be in danger," he warned him.

"I've been on duty since eight o'clock this morning. I ha-ven't seen her come in. It's the truth."

"Have you seen her friend, Charles?"

"No, sir. Come inside," he said, opening the door for Reed to pass. "The reporter. He's getting out of his car."

"This is an emergency, Ernesto," he said. "Can you get the key to her apartment so we can be sure she is not there?"

"Yes, sir. I will bring it up."

He went up ahead of Ernesto. When he got to her floor, he checked the light fixture, then the door. No key, and the door was locked. He knocked on the door and waited. No answer, not a sound could be heard from inside the apartment. He paced the hallway, knowing where he was going next if she wasn't there.

He looked up when the elevator dinged. He watched Ernesto step out with someone behind him. They both hurried down the hallway toward him.

"Who are you?" Reed asked the other man as they ap-proached him.

"Don Headley," the man with Ernesto answered. "Build-ing manager. I understand you are Ms. Maxwell's attorney?"

"I am, and I need to get in her apartment, so let's dispense with the niceties for now. Can we?"

"Certainly, sir," he said, sliding the key into the lock. "Ernesto explained that this is an emergency." He pushed the door open and stepped aside.

Reed sailed past him and called Jordan's name as he swept through her apartment. She wasn't there, and based on the last time he'd been there with her, it didn't look like she'd been back since. "Thank you," he said as he hurried back to the elevators.

"Sir, could I trouble you for a business card?" the manager asked, striding toward him while Ernesto locked the door behind them.

"Of course." He pulled one out of the inside pocket of his suit jacket and handed it to him. By the time the elevator arrived, Ernesto had joined them. "Do either of you know where the *Between the Pages* bookstore is?" he asked, rushing into the elevator.

Ernesto was the first to speak up as the doors closed behind them. "Yes, I do. You turn right outside the building. At the corner, you turn right again. It is about halfway down the block on the left."

"Thank you. Ernesto, will you call my office if you see Ms. Maxwell?"

"Yes, I will," he promised. "I hope you find her."

He nodded. When they reached the lobby floor and the doors parted, he flew out of the elevator and out the front door.

"Straight ahead and turn right at the corner," he instructed the driver as he pulled the car door shut behind him. "Pull over when you see the bookstore *Between the Pages* on the left."

He punched in Ben's number on his cell phone, and as they pulled out into traffic, he looked over his shoulder. The car with the reporter was following them.

"This is Ben."

"Ben, it's Reed. Did you check the numbers on the caller ID?"

"Yes. Two numbers were called today. The first is to *Between the Pages*, the second to the *Moonlit Inn*."

"I'm headed to the bookstore now. I want you to call the *Moonlit Inn* and see if Jordan made reservations there, but first, tell me what you found out from the concierge."

"Jordan left the building alone, about forty-five to fifty minutes before I got there. She got into a car, not a cab."

He glanced at his watch and calculated the time. She had left a little less than two hours ago. "All right. Get the home address for Charles Olgalvie from Harry. Call me back with it. Then plan on meeting me there. Tell Harry to find out what kind of car Olgalvie owns and to stay put."

"Yes, sir."

The car pulled to the curb. He knew it was a wasted effort to check the bookstore, but he had to cover all the bases. He didn't want to jump ahead and miss anything. "I'll be back in a minute," he said, exiting the car. He glanced back and noticed that the reporter's car had pulled to a stop a few yards behind his.

He ran across the street, dodging cars trying to move along in the traffic and eliciting a few horns and oaths. A rush of musty, stale air smacked into him as he pulled open the door to the bookstore. It wasn't much cooler in the small, dimly lit store than outside. He saw one customer browsing a shelf of discounted books and an ill-dressed man seated at the cash register.

"Herman Crane?" he asked, walking up to the register.

"Who's asking?" the man grumbled as he slid off the stool he had been occupying.

"I'm looking for Charles Olgalvie," Reed said, ignoring his

question.

"He ain't here," he said and returned to the stool.

"When did you see him last?"

The man looked him over. "Don't employees have privacy rights or something?"

Reed reached into his back pocket and pulled out his billfold. He slid a hundred-dollar bill out and set it on the counter. "I think they repealed that law."

"I think you're right," the man said as he slid the bill off the counter. "He left a couple of hours ago."

"Do you know where he went?"

"He didn't say."

"Did he say when he'd be back?"

"Nope, didn't say."

"What did he say?"

"Not much." He shrugged. "Just that he had an emergency to tend to."

"When's his next shift scheduled?"

"Tomorrow. He works every day, but I doubt he'll be here."

"What makes you think that?"

"He said he didn't know how soon he'd be able to make it back to work."

"What's his home address?"

"Just a minute." He pulled out a battered tablet from under the counter, opened it, and turned a few pages. He jotted something on the bottom of a page, ripped it out of the tablet, and handed it to Reed.

Reed took the paper, glanced down at the address scribbled on it, and tossed his business card on the counter. "Call me if you hear from him," he said before running out the door.

"If you see him first, tell him he's fired," the man called after him.

As he stepped off the curb, his phone rang. He answered it while he dashed back across the street. "What's the address?" he asked when he heard Ben's voice.

"It's in Brooklyn, Brownsville." Ben gave him the address. It matched the one he'd just gotten. "Harry says Olgalvie doesn't own a car. At least not one that's registered."

"If he did own one, I'm sure he didn't own it for long living in Brownsville." He ducked into his car. It pulled away from the curb as soon as he closed the door. "Head toward Brownsville," he told the driver. "Lose the car behind us first. I want you to meet me at the address in Brownsville," he said into the phone again. "Bring Ted Garner with you and Harry." At six-four, three-hundred-fifty pounds, and licensed to carry a gun, Harry would be good to have along in Brownsville, he figured.

"Who's Ted Garner?"

"An attorney in my office. What did you find out from the *Moonlit Inn*?"

"They didn't have any reservations under Jordan's name."

"Put Harry on the phone now and go get Garner. I'm on my way to Brownsville now."

"What do you need, Reed?" Harry asked. Reed could hear the eagerness in his voice. He always loved a good hunt.

"When you were doing your research on Olgalvie, did any address in Pennsylvania come up?"

"No, but we didn't check any records in Pennsylvania. Why?"

"I remember him telling Jordan he owned a place in Pennsylvania. He wanted to take her there. Call your office and get someone working on finding an address for him there. I don't think we're going to find him in Brownsville."

"I'll get right on it. Anything else?"

"Yes, you're going with Ben and Ted and meeting me at Olgalvie's apartment in Brownsville. Get moving."

"We're out the door," he said.

Within half an hour, they had converged at the apartment building in Brownsville. It was an old, dilapidated, three-story building housing about twelve apartments. "Olgalvie's is on the second floor," Harry said as they charged through the front door of the building.

Their footsteps echoed on the decrepit stairs amid the scramble of voices and music that spewed from the units as they clamored up to the second floor. A stench of foul smells laced with urine permeated the hall. Reed could almost feel Harry's adrenaline shoot through his own veins. When they reached Olgalvie's apartment, Reed hammered his fist against the door.

The door across the hall opened but then slammed shut when all four men turned to look.

Reed looked at Harry and half-grinned. "Would you like to try the door?"

Harry grinned back, then lifted a leg. He gave the door a hard, blunt kick, and it flung open, bounced against a wall, then off the frame and finally came to a rest, partially open.

"Well, would you look at that," Harry said. "The door is open. Someone must want us to go in. Gentlemen?" he said, moving aside.

A tidal wave of nausea slammed against Reed when he stepped inside.

"Oh. God." Reed heard the catch in Ted's voice as he choked on his words.

"This doesn't look good," Ben said. "Not good at all."

"Holy shit," Harry said from behind them.

Chapter Twelve

The walls were papered with pictures of Jordan. Manne-quins wearing photographs of her face were positioned around the room in various poses. Some were naked. One had a pair of gloves, another a pair of shoes. Probably Jordan's, Reed guessed. "Don't touch anything," he ordered, maneu-vering through the sea of trash on the floor. "Harry, let's check the rest of the apartment."

Harry drew his gun and waded through the trash ahead of Reed. Reed kicked aside a pizza box, and a rat sprang out and skittered away. Ben and Ted stood where they had entered. From the looks on their faces, Reed figured they were still ab-sorbing the horror and disgust.

He followed Harry from the living room, and Harry nod-ded toward a small kitchen on the right. Roaches swarmed piles of take-out containers that littered the counters and spilled onto the floor. A pair of socks hung from the door of a small microwave oven. With blotches of dark red stains, a shirt lay strewn across the sink, and a pair of pants lay crum-bled inside an open cabinet.

Across from the kitchen was a small bathroom encased in filth and mold. The toilet seat had been ripped from its hinges, and there was a hole in the ceiling where Reed assumed there was once a fan. Soiled towels hung from nails that had been driven into the wall.

Harry nodded toward a room a few steps past the kitchen. Reed followed him to it. Inside, a mattress lay on the floor. Reed swallowed hard to keep the contents of his stomach from coming up when he saw another mannequin spread eagle across the bed. "That sick, son-of-a-bitch," he said, the words oozing from his lips.

"That doesn't begin to describe him," Harry said, tucking his gun back into its holster. He squinted at something on the wall, then climbed over a pile of clothes and newspapers to get a closer look. "Yeah, I'd say we got our man."

Reed crossed the room and joined him near the newspaper and magazine clippings taped to the wall. Among them were a scattering of pictures of Jordan and Tanner. In each photo, Tanner's image had suffered a series of punctures. Reed watched Harry take a pen from his pocket and lift the corner of a picture. The puncture marks had penetrated the wall. "I'll bet a Buck knife did that." Harry tapped his pen against another photo. "And I'll bet you were next."

Reed recognized the photograph of him and Jordan. It was their engagement photograph that the papers had dug up and reprinted with one of the articles about Jordan. The same type of puncture marks marred his face in the picture. "It looks that way. It's too bad the asshole didn't come looking for me."

He snatched his cell phone from his pocket and punched in the direct number for the DA handling Jordan's case. His call was picked up on the third ring. He didn't wait for a voice. "Crocker, it's Reed Carrington. There's something you have to see. Right now."

"Hello to you, too, Carrington, and I'm in the middle of something."

"Whatever it is, it's not as important as this."

"As what?"

"I have the evidence that proves who killed Tanner."

"Look, Carrington, I know you were engaged to the lady, but I have all the evidence I need to prove she murdered Tanner."

"You aren't going to have the chance to prove it. Whether

you get down here or not, you'll have to dismiss the charges against her. Now, you can either get your ass down here and keep the egg off of your face, maybe even look like a hero, or watch you and your office look like incompetent fools on the eleven o'clock news."

"Where the hell is down here?"

"Brownsville." He gave him the address.

"I'm regretting this already."

"You'll be thanking me later. And you better bring some detectives from the Crime Scene Unit with you."

"Shit. This better be worth it if I have to bring troops with me."

"It is, but you better hurry if you don't want someone else to steal the press coverage." He hung up, maneuvered his way back through the trash, and started issuing orders. "Ted, you'll wait here for Crocker and fill him in when he gets here. If the press shows up before he gets here, handle them. Harry, you're going to head up to the *Moonlit Inn,* just in case. And, Harry, I assume you got an address in Pennsylvania for me?"

"Yeah." He was already pulling out a piece of paper. "It's in the Poconos. About three hours from here. The property is in the name of his parents, Sylvester and Mildred Olgalvie, but you won't be seeing them up there. They're both deceased."

"I hope to God we find her." He took the paper, noted the address, and then looked at his watch. "They probably aren't there yet, if that's where the asshole is headed."

"We could call the highway patrol and set up roadblocks," Ted suggested.

"No." Reed shook his head. "We don't know what kind of car they're in. They would spot the roadblock before the cops spot them."

"What about me?" Ben asked.

"You're coming with me," Reed replied as he headed toward the door. "Let's go."

"Get the bastard, Reed," Harry called after him. "And if I get him, I'll save a piece for you."

Jordan awoke groggy, a musty smell hanging heavy around her. The sound of a bird's chatter pierced the silence. It took a minute to remember that she'd been on her way to a quaint little inn in the Hudson Valley.

She pushed herself up and blinked the haze from her eyes. The room was dim, the dark paneled walls and dark-painted, plywood floor absorbing most of the light streaming in through the few windows. She'd been lying on an old sofa, the flowered fabric faded and worn. A floor lamp, missing its shade, stood at one end of the sofa.

A man's voice startled her and drew her attention to a chair, as equally faded and worn as the sofa, occupying a corner of the small room. "It's about time you woke up."

"Charles?" she managed, despite the chalky dryness in her throat. He was seated in the chair, watching her. His eyes are harsh and penetrating, almost angry, she thought, and an uneasy feeling crept over her.

"How are you feeling?" His voice was cold.

"Kind of tired. Where are we?" She rose slowly, gauging her balance. When she felt her legs steady under her, she took a few steps and glanced around. A small refrigerator, an old stove, and a sink atop a single cabinet lined the wall just inside a door that led outside. A crude rock fireplace was set in the opposite wall. The wall to one side of the chair where Charles sat contained two doors that she assumed led to other rooms. "What are we doing here?"

"You said you wanted to get away. Remember?"

"Yes, but you were supposed to drive me to the *Moonlit*

Inn."

"People would recognize you there," he said. "This is better. You have complete privacy."

She felt his stare follow her as she walked to a window. Beyond the bars crossing over them, there was nothing but forest. She remembered the coffee and wondered if he had put something in it to knock her out and if that was why she'd fallen asleep. A chill crawled over her as her mind questioned whether he would keep her against her will.

She strolled to another window and tried to make sense of the situation. Bars crossed over it, as well. "Why are there bars on the windows, Charles? Is it not safe here?"

"It's perfectly safe here. The bars are to keep the bears out when no one is here."

"Where are we that there are bears around?"

"We're in the mountains. There's nobody for miles around us."

"Who owns this place?"

"I do."

She sauntered over to the refrigerator, careful to conceal her uneasiness. She pulled the door open to see for how long a stay he had prepared. There were only a few sodas on a shelf. It was a good sign. She hoped. "Where will we eat dinner tonight? Are there restaurants nearby?"

"We should stay away from the restaurants. You wouldn't want to be seen."

"Then where will we eat?"

"Here. I'll get groceries for us later."

"That's very sweet of you, but I don't want to impose on you any more than I have."

She strolled back to the sofa under his frigid glare. It iced the chill already in her bones and deepened her uneasiness. "I think I'd like to go back to the city tonight. We could stop somewhere on the way back and have dinner."

"There's no need to go back. We have everything we need here." A hint of impatience, almost threatening, colored his voice. "And you don't need to worry about anybody ever finding you here."

The words fell over her like a dense, suffocating cloud. She got up and started for the door. "I want to go back." She struggled to keep her voice even. "Please, Charles, take me back." Her heart dropped like lead when she saw the deadbolt lock. She tried the door anyway, but it didn't budge.

"You can't go back. And you can't leave."

She spun around to face him. "Why are you doing this?" Her voice was a fusion of fear and anger as she felt her control slipping away.

"He's trying to take you away from me just like Steve Tanner tried to take you away. And I won't let him. I'll stop him just like I stopped Steve Tanner."

"You killed Steve?" The horror of it struck her like a fist to the heart and stole her next breath.

"Yes." A slight smile crossed over his face. "And I'll kill him, too."

"Who?" Breathe, she told herself. Try to stay calm. "Who are you talking about?"

"Your lawyer. You think he is trying to protect you. He isn't. He just wants you." The anger in his eyes slipped into his voice, and his fingers coiled into fists. "I saw you. The night it rained. I was watching you. I saw what he did to you."

Nausea churned in her stomach as his words loomed over her, and the panic inside her swelled. Before her eyes, the room moved in slow motion like one big wave. Breathe, she reminded herself. Stay alert. Think. She drew a slow breath, then released it. "Please take me back. I promise, no one will take me away from you."

"Words!" His back snapped ramrod straight with the

sharp climb in his voice. "Those are just words. You've already proven them to be untrue."

"Charles—"

"Liar!" he yelled and sprang from the chair. In an instant, his icy fingers were around her neck, his crazed eyes boring into hers. "Don't lie to me," he threatened between clenched teeth.

She stood motionless in his grasp, the fear ripping through her. He could easily snap her neck. She could die right there. Her life could end at that moment. She'd never see Reed again, and he would have no idea what had happened to her. He'd have no idea that she still loved him.

"Don't bother screaming. No one will hear you," he said with a dead calm, then released her.

She fell to her knees, clutching her neck, sucking in air. She listened to his footsteps thunder across the floor, then heard the click of a lock. The door opened with a creak, then slammed shut, and the lock clicked again. She waited until she heard him step down from the last porch step before she pushed herself up.

It was quiet outside. From where she was standing, she could see that he wasn't in the car. She approached the door, her gaze dancing from window to window for any sign of him. By the time she reached the door, she still hadn't spotted him. She knew it was a futile attempt, but she had to try. She closed her fingers around the door handle and gave it a hard yank. It didn't budge. She yanked it again, and again, willing it to break loose with each attack until she was almost breathless. She delivered one last assault with the heel of her shoe, then scrambled to a window.

The bars were spaced too closely to squeeze through. As she tugged on the lock and jerked the window up, she just prayed that at least one of the bars would be loose enough to kick free. She grabbed the bars and tried to wrestle them free.

They had been bolted in tight. She slammed the window down and tried another until she had tried them all.

There was no escape. She had no choice but to wait for him to return. She let the rage inside her percolate. She was going to need it and all the fury it could unleash to face him. Her mind raced to come up with some sort of a plan. She was going to have to make sure he'd be down for the count when she struck. She'd seen the knife sheath dangling from his belt.

The skids barely touched the ground before Reed and Ben sprang from the helicopter and sprinted the few hundred feet to the small airport terminal. Bursting through the door, Reed scanned the waiting area near the only gate. A handful of people were standing and sitting around, none of them wearing a sheriff's uniform.

"Hello there, gentlemen," a young woman in a crisp, white apron called out to them from behind a small dining counter. "Can I get you a cup of coffee? It's fresh."

"No, thanks," Reed said, starting toward her. "We're supposed to meet Sheriff Drummond here. Has he arrived yet?"

"Haven't seen him. I can call him and see if he's on his way if you want."

"Yes, I'd appreciate that," he said with a nod. "You can tell him Reed Carrington is here."

"Will do." She turned and took a few steps to a phone mounted on the wall. He watched her from the counter as she lifted the receiver and made the call. It took her less than a minute for her to return. "He apologizes for being late. Said he hit a deer and had to get another car. He said he'd be here in fifteen minutes. Would you like that coffee while you wait?"

"I can't wait." He turned to a few men hanging around the ticket counter. "Can any of you fellows give me a lift?"

They all turned toward him. An elderly man with a full head of white hair looked him over and then spoke. "I'd be happy to if it's not too far," he offered.

"It's not far, and I'll make it worth your while."

"I'm Earl," he said, shuffling over to him and thrusting out a hand. "Earl Sykes."

Reed took the old man's hand and received a hearty shake. "Reed Carrington."

"Where are we headed?" the old man asked.

"I need to get to a cabin on the west side of the lake." He pulled up a map on his cellphone and showed it to the old man. "I have an address. It's in this area." He pointed to a red circle on the map.

"No problem. I can get you there. How much you paying?"

"How fast can you get me there?"

"In a jiffy."

"Will a hundred do it?"

"You betcha. Let's go."

"Ben, wait for Sheriff Drummond to get here," he said as he turned to follow the old man. "Then get out to the cabin." He forwarded the map to Ben's cellphone, then caught up to the old man.

Earl didn't waste any time. With a few unlawful turns, speeds Reed was sure could land the old man in jail, and a couple of other illegal maneuvers, he guessed Earl had shaved off at least ten minutes from the drive, and for that, he gave him an extra hundred dollars.

"There's no telling from here just how far back the place is. Are you sure you don't want me to drop you off at the door?" Earl asked after Reed instructed him to pull to the side of the road. "You aren't exactly dressed for a hike, if you don't mind my saying so."

"I'm sure," he said, lifting the handle to the door of the old pick-up. "As I said, I want this to be a surprise."

"I'd be happy to wait in case your friend isn't there," he offered.

"That won't be necessary, Earl." He'd already heard from Harry. Jordan hadn't shown up at the *Moonlit Inn*, and he was pretty sure she wasn't going to. He stepped down from the truck. "You can head out now," he said, shutting the door. "Thanks for the ride."

He started down the gravel driveway at a steady jog. He figured the woods were thick enough on either side so that if he heard a car, he could duck behind a tree and avoid being seen. Stones crunched under the soles of his *Prada's* for a half mile before the cabin came into view. It was about a quarter of a mile further down. There was an older model *Buick* parked out front.

He felt as if he'd been given a shot of caffeine straight to the heart as the adrenalin kicked in. Jordan was there. He knew it. He could feel her.

He stopped close to the edge of the trees and studied the cabin. A chimney jutted up from behind it. There could be windows on either side of the chimney, but he figured it was unlikely from the size of the cabin. He decided that approaching from the rear would be his best approach and ducked into the forest to circle around.

He stayed low and crept through the thick woods, dodging low-hanging branches and poison ivy and keeping the cabin within his sight. There was no sign of life inside or out. The windows were all closed, at least in the front and on the one side, and there were no lights on. He wondered if Jordan was tied up. He remembered the mannequins and felt his jaw tighten at the image.

He inched the rest of the way, careful to keep his footing among the fallen twigs and branches until he was at the back of the cabin. Crouched down, he peered between two limbs. He'd been right. There were no windows on the rear wall.

He tensed at the sound of a slight rustling in the leaves behind him and realized how unprepared he was to be tromping through the woods hunting down a murderer. Still, he was sure he could handle the son of a bitch as long as he could catch him by surprise.

On the other hand, the little prick could have grown up running all through these woods. He imagined Charles could run through them blind with minimal sound if that was the case. A bead of sweat dripped down his neck at the thought that the asshole might be standing behind him, poised to pounce.

He lowered his head and turned it a few inches. Ready to spring, he slid his gaze over the ground behind him. He froze when he recognized the chestnut-colored bands. They were the markings of a copperhead snake. It wasn't more than an arm's length away and twice that length. He didn't know much about snakes, but he knew the little shit was poisonous.

He moved away, and when he was sure he was out of striking distance, he crawled toward the clearing behind the cabin. At its edge was a mound of unsplit logs and uncut branches. He surveyed the pile, ensuring there were no snakes around it, and picked up a limb. It was about twice the length of a baseball bat, just as thick, still a little green, and solid enough to withstand a good whack. It would do.

Clutching the branch, he darted the few steps across the clearing to the rock wall of the fireplace. He slipped around to the side of the cabin and crept up to the window. The heavy iron bars made the place a virtual prison for anyone inside, and they were going to make it a hell of a lot more challenging to get Jordan out. He felt his fingers tighten around the branch and vowed that if that psychotic son-of-a-bitch hurt her, he would tear him apart, limb by limb.

There was no sign of anyone inside as far as he could see, but from the angle of his position, he figured he could see only about a third of the cabin. As he bent down to pass under the window, a blinding pain pierced his right shoulder as something drove deep through flesh and muscle and was ripped back out. He released a gut-wrenching yell as he turned, ready to strike, and met a crushing blow against his left temple. His vision blurred, and his legs buckled under him. He collapsed to the ground in darkness.

CHAPTER THIRTEEN

The cry of agony ripped over Jordan's flesh like a cleaver and had her bolting from her hiding place. She sprinted to the window and threw it open. Her heart stopped for a second and then, with a jolt, skyrocketed to blinding speed when she saw Reed lying in a pool of blood beneath the window. Charles was standing over him, blood glistening on the blade of his knife. "Noooooo!" she screamed, yanking on the iron bars. "You bastard!"

His crazed stare shot up to her before he took off in a sprint. She watched through the windows as he darted around the corner to the front of the cabin. When she heard the lock turn, she dashed toward the sofa. Her hand was within inches of the floor lamp when she was jerked backward, a handful of her hair tangled in the knuckles of Charles's hand.

"Let go of me!" she shrieked, planting her nails deep into his wrist.

He cried out in pain, releasing the handful of hair.

It was all she needed as she clamored for the lamp and clamped her fingers around it. She could hear his heavy panting behind her, readying for a second attack. She lifted the lamp and swung. He leaped away, and she missed him, the lamp's base landing against the sofa. He moved fast toward her, and she lashed out again, but couldn't get the same momentum.

He kicked the lamp from her hands as it sailed past him. "You ungrateful bitch," he spat, charging toward her.

She screamed as his hand closed around her throat.

Reed awoke to Jordan's scream, pain ricocheting inside his head, agony slicing through his shoulder. He reached for the branch that lay beside him and cringed. He tried again, this time clutching it with his left hand. He struggled to his feet and took an unsteady step, stumbling against the cabin. A shock wave of pain ripped through him. The pain he could endure, but the weakness was sucking the life from him. He steadied himself and, fighting the weakness, staggered the rest of the way until he reached the front of the cabin.

The door was open. He could see Charles, his back to him, leaning over Jordan, bearing down on her. The knife was in one hand, dangling at his side. His other hand was clasped around her throat, and she was on her knees.

Rage shot through Reed's veins, pumping the life back into him. He squeezed his fingers around the branch, took the two porch steps, and lunged through the front door. He wielded the limb in one quick, powerful motion with every ounce of strength he had left. The branch struck Charles across the skull with a whack, and he released Jordan on his way down.

Struggling, she pushed herself up and stumbled toward Reed, fighting for her next breath.

Charles scrambled to his feet and charged toward them, the knife still in his hand.

Jordan wrapped her hands around Reed's, still holding the branch. She helped him lift it as Charles hurdled toward them. He rammed into the end of it and fell to the floor, yanking it from their hands on the way down. He staggered to his feet and charged at them again.

Reed lifted an arm across Jordan and stepped in front of her. His strength depleted, he stood powerless as Charles raised the knife, ready to slash him to pieces.

A gun blast went off behind them, the knife dropped, and

Charles fell to the floor writhing in pain from a gunshot wound to the thigh.

"I suggest you stay down this time, boy," Sheriff Drummond said from behind Reed. He shot off orders for a couple of ambulances and a deputy.

"I got you," Ben said, locking an arm around Reed.

"I'm . . . glad . . ." Reed managed, his words slurring and his feet faltering. His shirt was drenched with blood, and he could feel himself slipping away.

"Don't let him fall." Jordan's voice was raspy, and the panic in it was unmistakable. "Ben, hold on to him," she cried as she tried to help Ben keep him from going down.

"I got him." He grabbed Reed's left arm and stepped under it, catching him before he collapsed. "I got him," he repeated as they struggled the few feet to the sofa.

"He's lost a lot of blood," Jordan said. "And he's still bleeding. We have to stop it."

Reed fought through the haze as he watched Sheriff Drummond clamp a pair of cuffs over Charles's wrists and then hurry toward them. He helped Ben lower him to the sofa.

"Okay, little lady, why don't you see if there are some clean towels in the bathroom," Sheriff Drummond told Jordan.

"Hold on to him, son," he said to Ben as he tugged Reed's shirt from his trousers. Once loose, he ripped it apart and peeled it from his back. "That's a nasty one, all right."

Jordan returned with a towel in her hands. He felt them trembling as she pressed it to his shoulder. The pain shot through him, assaulting every exposed, raw nerve.

"Good, hold it there," Sheriff Drummond said. "Ben, can you keep him sitting up? It's best if he doesn't lie down."

"Yeah." He could hear sirens in the distance. "No problem."

"Okay. I'll be right back." Those were the last words he heard.

The harsh fumes of smelling salts brought Reed back. He lifted his head with a grumble. His eyes flickered open, and he grimaced in pain.

"That's it, buddy," Sheriff Drummond said. "Hang in there. Help is on the way."

"Jordan . . . where's . . . Jordan?" he mumbled.

"I'm here." Her voice came from behind him. "I'm right here."

The next twenty-four hours passed in a dense fog. Reed wasn't even sure where he was until he woke up at seven o'clock, according to the clock on the wall, the following evening and recognized the stark, sterile surroundings of a hospital room. When he tried to lift his head, his memory came flooding back. With a moan, he let his head drop back into the pillow.

"How are you feeling, dearie?" Mrs. Doyle asked from somewhere in the room.

"Mrs. Doyle?" He struggled to find his voice.

"Yes, dearie, it's me." She got up and strolled over to the bed. "You had yourself quite an adventure, I heard."

"I guess you could call it that. How did you find out? What are you doing here?"

"Jordan called me. She told me what happened to you and asked me to come here and sit with you."

"Where is she?"

"Home, I suppose," she said, placing the palm of her hand on his forehead. "I thought I would stop by your apartment in the city and pick you up some clean clothes to wear when the doctors let you leave. Seems your office needed straightening up."

He let out a low groan, remembering the files Jordan had found.

"That's right." She pursed her lips as she peered down at him. "Shame on you, keeping those files someplace she could so easily come across. I hope you have a backup plan."

He had a plan. And it was quite simple.

Jordan had been home for a week in peace and quiet. She had tried to write, then tried to read, but hadn't been able to keep her mind off of everything that had happened over the past months. Ben had filled her in on how Reed had found out about Charles and what they'd found in his apartment. It had made her sick to her stomach to hear about it, and she tried not to think about it. She was also dealing with the guilt of Steve Tanner's death. She might not have put the knife in his chest, but she sure as hell took the blame. If not for her friendship with Charles, Steve Tanner would still be alive.

She still had no idea who had left the scarf in her apartment. For all she knew, the scarf could have been left by Charles for some twisted reason. She had no doubt that he was the one who had moved the photographs in her office and had gone through the boxes in the spare room. In any event, since he was in custody and nothing had been stolen, there seemed to be no reason to be concerned about it.

According to the attorney from Reed's firm, the district attorney's office had dropped all the charges against her. Her case was closed, and, except for the bill she was waiting for from Reed's firm, the criminal case was behind her.

She combed her fingers through her hair and let her head fall back against the chair. Everything that had happened at the cabin had proven that any suspicions she'd had about Reed after finding the files had been wrong. He had nothing to do with Steve Tanner's murder, but he'd tried to hurt her, and she couldn't help but think that his offer to represent her was somehow intended to end up hurting her.

Despite knowing that, she had wanted to stay with him after she and Ben had taken him to the hospital. She'd wanted to take care of him until she was sure he was healed. It had taken every ounce of willpower to call Mrs. Doyle to do it instead and to tear herself away from Reed. There'd been no point in her staying. The case was over, and so was their relationship, for a second time.

She looked at the clock and sighed. It was almost noon, and she hadn't showered, hadn't managed to write even a word for the article she was working on, and hadn't paid a single invoice from the stack of bills sitting on her desk. All she'd managed to do was drag herself out of bed, throw on a robe, then settle into her reading chair. Maybe another cup of coffee would get her going.

She pushed herself up from the chair and strolled into the kitchen. Her apartment had never felt so enormous or empty, and she had never felt so alone. She'd avoided the flood of phone calls from friends, the media, and who knew who else. She didn't feel up to talking to anybody or having any guests.

The shrill of her telephone jolted her from her thoughts. She looked at the caller ID. It was Reed's office. She answered it.

"Ms. Maxwell, this is Rose Higgins, Mr. Carrington's secretary. Mr. Carrington asked me to call you to see if you could come in this afternoon around two o'clock."

"He's back in the office already?" she asked, surprised. The knife had penetrated deep and through the muscle. The blow to his head had caused a concussion and quite a bit of swelling. He'd lost a lot of blood and required many stitches. She couldn't imagine anyone bouncing back from injuries like his so soon.

"No. He won't be back for a few more weeks. He's coming in only for this meeting."

"Mr. Garner already told me the district attorney's office

has dropped all of the charges against me." She didn't need to go to Reed's office just to hear it from him.

"Yes, I understand that's true. All of the charges have been dropped. Mr. Carrington didn't tell me why he needs you to come in, but I imagine there are a few things that need to be taken care of before your file is officially closed."

"All right," she agreed. If there were loose ends to tie up, she supposed it was better to get them done sooner rather than later. She didn't want to drag out anything that might be needed to close her case with the DA's office. "Please let Mr. Carrington know I can be there at two."

"Very good, thank you."

She set the receiver down and wondered why he had Rose call instead of calling himself, then shrugged off the thought. Rose was his secretary. That was her job. She was sure he had moved on from her case, other than taking care of whatever matter was left to officially close her file, and had moved on from her.

She had let her guard down. She'd fallen in love with him all over again. Despite her warnings to herself to keep her distance, stay out of the past, and be careful, she'd allowed herself to be downright reckless. Now, she was paying for it.

She decided on water rather than coffee and pulled a bottle of sparkling water out of the refrigerator. She poured it into a glass and headed toward the bathroom. It was noon. She had enough time to take a long, relaxing bath before facing Reed again.

An hour later, she was standing in her closet and frowning as she stared at a pair of slacks. They were too casual, and the red dress next to them was too dressy. Everything was either too simple or too formal. She pulled out a plain black skirt and a white blouse and decided that they were just going to have to do. She slid her feet into a pair of red pumps and pulled a matching red clutch from the shelf. She surveyed the look in the mirror and, satisfied, headed for Reed's office.

She was escorted to his suite when she arrived.

"Ms. Maxwell, thank you for coming on such short notice," Rose said. "I'll let Mr. Carrington know you're here."

"Thank you," she replied and waited while Rose buzzed him. She heard him answer, and then Rose escorted her in.

"Hello, Jordan," Reed said with a smile as he walked toward her. "It's nice to see you again."

His voice flowed over her like warm caresses. "Thank you. You're looking better," she managed. The truth was, he was looking much better, all things considered. She guessed that he was carrying his arm in a sling, most likely to minimize movement to his shoulder. The swelling to his head had subsided but was replaced by a dark bruise that covered an entire eye. "How are you feeling?"

"Good. Come in, please," he said and ushered her toward his desk.

She noticed a woman sitting in one of the client chairs. She appeared very poised and elegantly dressed. As she approached her, the woman stood and smiled. She didn't recognize her and wondered who she was and why she was there for her meeting with Reed.

"Jordan, I would like to introduce you to Victoria Carr," Reed said. "Victoria, this is Jordan Maxwell."

Jordan accepted her hand. "It's nice to meet you," she said.

"Thank you, and it's a joy to finally meet you," Victoria replied.

"Excuse me, but are you related to Congressman Carr?"

"Yes. I'm his wife," she answered.

"Why don't we all move over to the sitting area," Reed suggested. "I think it will be more comfortable."

Jordan looked at Reed for some indication of why she was

meeting with Victoria Carr as they made their way across his office, but all he offered was a smile.

"May I get either of you a cup of coffee or a glass of water?" he asked once they had reached the sitting area.

"Nothing for me, thank you," Jordan replied, taking a seat.

"No, thank you," Victoria said as she sat down next to her.

"All right," Reed said, lowering himself to the chair across from them. "Let me know if either of you changes your mind."

"Jordan," Victoria began, her voice filled with trepidation. "Reed called me to tell me he wanted to return something to me that I had lost. And he also wanted to know why it had been found in your apartment."

"The scarf?" She could hear the shock in her words as her mind filled with questions. "I don't understand."

"Yes, the scarf." Victoria nodded. "I told Reed how it had gotten in your apartment and why I was there, and I asked him if he would let me explain it to you, personally." She glanced at Reed, then back at her. "And he agreed."

Jordan turned to Reed. His eyes told her nothing, and all he offered was a reassuring nod. "All right. I would like to know," she said, returning to Victoria.

"Before I explain, I'd like to apologize to you. I'm sorry I went to your apartment without your permission." She lowered her gaze and, appearing uncomfortable, shifted in her chair before continuing. "I know that was an unforgivable intrusion on your privacy, and I didn't intend to scare you or cause you any concern. That would be the last thing I would ever want to do."

Jordan nodded. "All things considered, finding the scarf and knowing someone had been in my apartment weren't the worst things I've experienced recently."

"I know." She reached over, placed a hand on Jordan's, and then lifted her gaze. "And I'm so sorry for all you've been through."

"Does your being in my apartment have anything to do with Charles Olgalvie?"

She shook her head. "I've never met him, but I feel responsible for everything that has happened. I put the wheels in motion."

"Are you talking about Steve Tanner's murder?"

"Yes." Her gaze dropped, and she drew her hand from Jordan's. "I suppose I should start from the beginning." She hesitated, and Reed stood. He gave her a nod, then strolled over toward the windows. She lifted her gaze back to Jordan and continued. "When I was seventeen, I was a fan of Steve Tanner." A slight smile graced her face. "A big fan. I was lucky enough to get backstage passes to one of his concerts. After the concert, I was lucky enough to be invited to a private party with his band. After that night, Steve and I had a brief relationship, if one could even call it that. It lasted a couple of weeks. When he went on tour, it ended."

"Does this have anything to do with his biography?" Her mind was racing as she tried to understand what Victoria was telling her. "Were you afraid your affair would be in the book?"

She paused for a second and took a slow breath. "I knew he told you that he wanted you to write his biography, but I wasn't concerned that our affair would be disclosed." She took another slow breath, then continued. "Shortly after Steve went on tour, I found out I was pregnant. I didn't know what to do. I finally told my mother. By that time, I was six months along. My mother was furious. She wanted to pretend like the pregnancy didn't exist. She made me stay at our house in Connecticut until I had the baby. I stayed there with a midwife, and she delivered my baby. Against my mother's orders, she let me hold the baby. She even let the baby stay with me through the night. The next morning, she left, and she took my baby with her. The day after that, I was picked up and brought back to New York."

"I'm sorry. That must have been difficult for you," Jordan said. "Steve mentioned that he'd recently found out about another child he'd fathered, but he didn't disclose any details."

She nodded. "It was tough. My mother never mentioned the pregnancy or my baby again, but I thought about my baby every day of my life. The nurse had taken a picture of her. It was a girl. And she had mailed it to me, at school, so my mother wouldn't know. Every day I looked at that picture, and I wondered where my baby had been taken, if she was healthy, if she was happy."

"You don't have to tell me any of this, Victoria. I'm no longer going to write Steve's biography."

"Yes. I need to tell you. My father died about a year ago. I never knew that he'd known about the baby, but he'd known everything. He even knew her parents and where she lived, and he told me just before he died. I was so happy to finally know my baby's name and where she lived. I wanted to reach out to her, but I made the mistake of telling my husband about her." She looked down and shook her head. "He was furious that I never told him about my baby. He forbade me from having anything to do with her. He said it would ruin his political career."

Jordan slid her hand over Victoria's. "I'm so sorry."

"Thank you," she replied and met Jordan's gaze. "I was devastated. I had wondered for so long about my baby, and here I had the chance to contact her, maybe even meet her. I couldn't just do nothing." She took Jordan's hand in hers. "So I made a plan to find out more about her. I called Steve and told him about her. I asked him if he would get in touch with her, meet with her, and tell me all about her. And I asked him not to tell her he was her father. I was afraid that if he did, she'd find out that I was her mother, and then everyone would find out. I was afraid . . ." She shook her head. "I was afraid it would ruin my husband's career."

The shock plowed through Jordan as she pulled her hand from Victoria's and found herself standing up, staring down at her. "What are you saying? Are you saying . . ." She couldn't finish the words. It was all too overwhelming. It was all too much. She had never been told that she had been adopted.

"Yes." Victoria stood and took a step toward her. "You are my and Steve's daughter."

"Reed?" She turned to look for him, and he had already returned and was at her side.

"Yes. You were adopted. I've verified it. I have the documents." He lifted a hand to her shoulder. "I talked to your uncle. Your parents were told that your birth parents were dead, so they didn't see the need to tell you that you were adopted, and they didn't want you to feel like you weren't their child or that you didn't belong with them."

Their words were like a bomb blasting through her, shattering her life. Everything she knew, everything she was, was a lie. She had no idea lies had been told, secrets had been kept. She combed her fingers through her hair, walked to the window, and stared out over the city, seeing none of it below her. "Oh, my God," she managed, barely a whisper. Steve Tanner had died in her arms, and she'd had no idea that he was her father. She turned to Victoria. "I . . . I don't know what to think about all of this. I don't know what to say." Her mind was a jumbled mess. "Why were you in my apartment?" she asked, not knowing why she had uttered the words. Of everything that had happened, that mattered the least.

Victoria's eyes were a mix of sorrow and regret. "It was difficult to speak with Steve. We couldn't meet, and it was mostly impossible to reach him by phone. We . . . I decided that since you were spending so much time with him, that I'd go to your apartment. I asked him if he could get me keys to your apartment, and he had them delivered to me. I went there hoping to find photo albums, scrapbooks, anything that would tell me about you and your life." She lowered her gaze. "I'm so sorry things turned out as they did. I had no idea anything like this would happen. Please don't hate me, Jordan."

She saw a tear roll down Victoria's cheek and walked back to her. "I don't hate you, Victoria, and I don't blame you for the acts of a mad man. But . . . this is all so shocking and overwhelming. I don't know . . . I just don't know what to think about any of it."

Reed pulled a kerchief from the pocket of his trousers and handed it to Victoria. He put a reassuring arm around her. "Victoria, I think Jordan just needs some time for all of this to sink in and to process it all."

"Yes, of course. I understand." She dabbed at her tears and forced a smile. "Thank you, Reed, for being here and letting me explain all of this to Jordan."

"You're welcome." He lowered his arm and slid his gaze to Jordan. "I know this isn't easy for either of you."

"Jordan, I know I have no right to expect anything from you." Victoria lifted a hand to her face and touched her fingers to her cheek. "But if you think you can ever forgive me, I would like to see you. I mean . . . if it's possible . . . I'd like to spend some time with you."

"I'll keep that in mind," she replied.

"Thank you." She drew her hand back, turned to Reed, and extended it to him. "Thank you, Reed. I should probably go now."

"It was very nice to see you again, Victoria." He took her hand and held it in his. "Please, let me walk you out."

Jordan returned to the window and stared out over the city. It looked different. It felt different.

"Are you all right?" Reed asked when he returned.

"Well, that was a lot to learn," she replied. "But, I think I'll be all right."

"I know it was a lot." He peered out the window. "Can I get you anything?"

"No, thank you." She shook her head. "How did you find out Victoria owned the scarf?"

"You're not going to believe it," he said, turning to her.

"Try me." She looked up at him and grinned. "I don't think there's much more that will surprise me."

He returned the grin with a nod. "I suppose not. Blair told me. She bought the scarf for Victoria."

"Hmm. I was wrong. That does surprise me. How did she even know we had the scarf and that we were trying to find who it belonged to?"

"It was on my desk when she came in for a visit. She recognized it and wanted to know why Victoria had been in to see me."

"When was that?"

"The morning that everything happened at the cabin. I didn't find out the rest until yesterday."

"Did you ever find out who broke into your office?"

"No. My computer wasn't found at Olgalvie's apartment or his cabin. I suspect Gary Carr had something to do with that, maybe trying to find out if I knew about Victoria and Tanner and whether I was planning on using it in your defense."

"Did you ask Victoria if she knew anything about that?"

"No. She feels bad enough about everything that's happened. Besides, I don't think Gary Carr confides in his wife much."

"Well, I guess other than that, we have all the pieces to the puzzle." She turned from the window and strolled toward the door. "I suppose we can both get back to our lives now."

"Not quite," he said. "We're not finished yet."

Chapter Fourteen

Jordan turned back. "There's more?"

"Oh, there's definitely more," Reed said, meeting her gaze. He slid his free hand in his trouser pocket and strode toward her. "For starters, I owe you an explanation. And an apology."

"Is this about the files?"

"Yes. It's about the files." He hadn't settled on the words, though he had thought about the conversation almost every waking moment over the past three days. He was just going to have to swallow his pride, for once, he decided. Keeping it had cost him five years without her. He stopped when he reached her and looked down at her. "When you left me five years ago, I thought for certain you would come back. I thought you'd realize that you were wrong to let Blair's behavior affect you so deeply and come between us."

"It wasn't just—"

He lifted the hand from his pocket. "Please, let me finish. I've been waiting a long time to say this."

She nodded. "Okay."

"When you didn't come back, it was like a slap in the face. Actually, it was more than that. I couldn't believe that our relationship meant so little to you that you would throw it all away because of some ridiculous stunt of Blair's. What she says and what she does means very little to me. I would have never survived her if I didn't let what she says and what she does slide off my back. I guess I expected you to do the same. And I couldn't understand why you didn't. I couldn't understand why you let what she did destroy our relationship." He took a step and paced around her. "I was hurt and angry, and I wanted you to feel as miserable as I did. So, when you started dating again, I paid your dates to stop asking you out. As time went on and the hurt and anger waned, I could justify it." He stopped and turned back to her. "I figured that if someone could walk away from you for a mere ten grand, they didn't deserve you in the first place."

"And your offer to represent me? Your insistence that I stay in Water Mill? Was that all just another plan to hurt me?"

"When I saw the news the morning you were arrested, my only thought was that I had to do everything possible to get you out of your situation. I couldn't risk letting you hire someone else. I couldn't risk someone else making any mistakes, screwing up your case, and you ending up in prison. I knew I was your best chance to keep your freedom." He paused for a moment and then continued. "It was after that I realized it was also an opportunity to make you fall in love with me again, an opportunity to make you regret that you had walked away from me. But there was a major flaw with that theory." He took a step toward her. "I didn't appreciate that despite the fact that five years had passed between us that I was still very much in love with you."

They both turned as the door to his office swung open, and Blair pranced in, Rose's assistant rushing in behind her. "I'm sorry, Mr. Carrington. She didn't give me a chance to announce her."

"It's all right. I understand."

The assistant nodded and left, closing the door behind her.

"Hello, my darling, how are you feeling today?" Blair said as she sashayed toward Reed and ignored Jordan. She lifted a hand to his cheek. "You look pale. You should be home, not here working."

"I'm feeling better, Blair, and I'm not working. But I am in the middle of something."

She slid her gaze to Jordan. "It's Jordan, isn't it?"

"Yes." She nodded. "Good afternoon, Mrs. Carrington."

"Would you mind too terribly being on your way?" she asked with a dismissive wave. "I need to speak with my son privately."

Jordan looked up at Reed. She didn't need to tell him what she was thinking. He could read it in her eyes. He turned his gaze to Blair. She was obviously not happy that Jordan was in his office. She isn't going to like what I'm about to say, either, he thought.

"Jordan isn't going anywhere, Blair," he answered for her, fighting hard to keep the anger from his voice. "And if you're going to speak to her, I expect you to do so with the respect that she deserves."

"I know Jordan is a client, but I cannot help but feel a little bitter toward the person who nearly got my son killed."

"She didn't nearly get me killed. It was my own stupidity that nearly got me killed. And not that it matters, but Jordan is no longer my client. In case you haven't heard, all of the charges against her were dismissed."

She released an annoyed sigh. "If she is no longer your client, what difference on earth does it make how I address her?"

"It matters because Jordan is going to be my wife."

"What?" The shock on Jordan's face was unmistakable, and he hoped she'd agree to marry him. It wasn't how he'd intended to ask her, but at least she wouldn't have to worry about what Blair would think or do once she found out. As far as he was concerned, Blair wasn't going to be a problem this time around. He was going to nip any problems with Blair in the bud.

"I'm not going to take no for an answer, and I'm not going to let anyone get in the way this time."

"I was told you were here, Blair," Aldrich said, strutting

through the door. "Ah, Jordan," he said, a smile cracking over his face. "How nice it is to see you, and congratulations on getting through this mess."

"Thank you, Mr. Carrington," Jordan replied, returning the smile.

"Aldrich," Blair said, her voice demanding his attention. "Reed has just announced that he intends to marry this woman. What do you think of that?"

"I think it's wonderful," he replied. "And it's about damn time. Welcome to the family, Jordan." He leaned in and kissed her on the cheek. "Congratulations, son," he added, giving Reed a pat on the shoulder.

"I absolutely will not allow this woman to marry into this family," Blair declared.

"Who I marry is not your choice." Reed's voice was firm and delivered the message. "And there is nothing you can do about it. I will not let you sabotage my wedding again."

"She's not worthy of the Carrington name. She could never live up to our standards."

"For God's sake, Blair," Aldrich cut in. "The only standards this family has are low ones. Your sister's a raging alcoholic, your brother has an illegitimate child with a stripper, my sister's cheating on her husband, your niece is on her third husband at only twenty-six years old, and your nephew's in a drug rehab facility for the fourth time. Hell, need I go on? This family should consider it a privilege to have Jordan in it. If anything, she should be running for the hills to get as far away from this family as possible."

"How dare you bring up such personal matters," she huffed. "They are private, and they have no bearing whatsoever on this situation."

"Don't make me choose between you and Jordan, Blair," Reed warned her.

She sidled up to Jordan, her lips lifting to a sneer. "Do you really think you deserve to be a Carrington?" Her words were laced with ice.

Jordan lifted a hand to Reed. "It's all right." She turned to Blair. "Mrs. Carrington, I've endured the deaths of the parents who raised me, I watched my birth father die a violent death, and I was charged with his murder. I was almost eaten alive by an angry mob, was kidnapped, and watched the man I love nearly bleed to death. With all due respect, there's nothing you can ever say or do to me that's any worse than what I've been through. I'm going to marry Reed." She softened her voice just a notch as she continued. "And you are welcome to come to the wedding if you'd like. It's your choice, but regardless of what you decide, the wedding will occur."

"Hmm." She dragged her gaze over Jordan. "If you think you can handle me, perhaps you are fit to be a part of this family." She thrust her gaze onto her husband. "Aldrich, let's go. We have reservations."

Reed slid an arm around Jordan's waist. "Well, Ms. Maxwell," he said after the door closed behind Aldrich. "It looks like we have a wedding to plan."

"Did it occur to you that I might not accept your proposal, Mr. Carrington?" she asked, sliding her arms around his neck.

"Not for a moment," he said with a grin. "I knew you wouldn't want to disappoint Mrs. Doyle."

"Does she know you intended to ask me to marry you?"

"Apparently, she's known all along. Now, let's make this official," he said, tucking his hand in his pocket and pulling out a diamond ring. He lifted her hand and slid it on her finger.

"Is this the same ring? Have you kept this ring all these years?"

"What was I supposed to do with it? I bought it for you." His lips curved into a grin. "I couldn't return it. It was humiliating enough being left at the altar."

"I didn't leave you at the altar," she protested.

"It doesn't matter. I'm going to tether you to it this time."

Chapter Fifteen

Jordan blinked the sleep from her eyes, her mind racing with all she had to do. Her lips lifted to a smile when she saw Reed propped up on an arm staring down at her.

"What are you doing?" she asked, tossing the covers aside. "We have a million things to do to get ready for this afternoon."

"Uh-uh," he replied, pulling the covers back over her, sliding an arm around her, and scooting her into him. "Relax. We've been planning this day for nine months." He skimmed his lips over hers. "The wheels are in motion. Let the people we've hired do their jobs. They don't need us." He let his lips wander down to her neck. "All we have to do is show up, and that's not for another eight hours."

"You know," she said, gliding her fingers down his chest. "You aren't even supposed to be here. The groom isn't supposed to see the bride the morning of the wedding."

"It's too late for that," he whispered, dragging his tongue over her breast.

"Mm," she cooed as his touch triggered little wisps of lust inside her. She continued the journey down to his penis and closed her fingers around him. "It appears so."

"I think all of our bad luck is behind us, anyway." He slid a hand between her legs, and the tiny wisps started to whip through her like a warm, summer wind.

"Yes," she managed, her ability to speak overwhelmed by physical needs. She rolled on top of him. When she spread her legs, he slipped inside her, and the heat between them soared.

She took him whole, then retreated, and retook him. Each movement was intense. Each motion was to be savored. And each action had a purpose. Each was intended to push him to the limits of his sanity. When he grabbed her hips and ground into her, she knew she had done that, and when the flames sliced through her, she knew she had gone there herself.

"I can't believe that I'm going to watch my daughter walk down the aisle on her wedding day," Victoria gushed, tears glistening in her eyes.

"I'm happy you're here," Jordan said, taking her hands in hers. Victoria had proven to be an essential part of her life. She had eased the pain and filled the loneliness that had plagued her since her mother had died, and she'd been invaluable with helping her orchestrate her wedding. She knew every event planner, chef, caterer, florist, musician, designer, photographer, printer, and every other type of person needed to plan a wedding. She had also put to rest any remaining doubts Blair might have had about her worthiness to be a Carrington. Apparently, the fact that Victoria Carr's blood flowed through her veins was enough to place her in the ranks of high society.

"Thank you for letting me be such a big part of this day, and thank you for including David. He's so thrilled to be one of Reed's groomsmen."

"I'm glad he's been so accepting of everything. I'm just sorry for all the trouble this has caused between you and your husband." She still didn't know who had leaked to the press that Victoria was her birth mother, but she wouldn't put something like that past Blair.

"It's been a blessing in disguise. David and I are much happier now. I should have left Gary a long time ago." Victoria squeezed Jordan's hands. "Let's not talk about it now. I don't want anything to dampen your wedding day."

"Jordan," her cousin called out as she waltzed through the door with Steve Tanner's two daughters, her half-sisters. "You look so beautiful."

Victoria stepped aside as they crowded around Jordan.

"The dress looks exquisite on you," Ali cried, the older of Steve's daughters. "Turn around. Let me see the whole thing. It's been so long since you ordered it that I forgot what it looks like."

Jordan did a quick spin.

"Oh, look at the buttons down the back. That is so striking," Sky chimed in, his other daughter.

"You all look so gorgeous," Jordan returned. "You're going to upstage me."

"Don't you worry about that," her cousin replied. "All eyes are going to be on you."

"Cole wants us to let you know he was able to get back in time to make it today. He's downstairs now," Ali said.

"Oh, I'm so glad. You all are going to make me cry and mess up my makeup." Jordan took Ali's hand and reached for Sky's. "I can't believe how wonderful you and your brother have been to me."

"Our brother," Sky corrected her. "You're a part of Dad, making you a part of our family. Dad wanted us to spend time with you and get to know you. We didn't know why at the time, but it became clear to us when we found out you're his daughter."

"It's always been important to Dad that all of his children get along," Ali said. "And that we all know we can rely on each other. And that includes you."

"Hello, everyone," Blair sang as she strutted through the door. "I want to see Jordan before the ceremony begins. You look lovely," she said as she looked her over and gave her an air kiss.

"Thank you," Jordan replied.

"Okay, ladies," Mrs. Doyle shouted above the chatter. "It's time for a wedding. Mrs. Carrington, Mrs. Carr, the ushers are waiting to take you to your seats. And lasses," she said, turning toward the bridesmaids. "You need to go line up downstairs and get ready."

"Okay, we're going," Ali replied as she led the other girls from the room.

"Slow down, girls," Blair called after them. "I have to be escorted to my seat first."

"You're so beautiful," Victoria said, adjusting Jordan's veil.

"I'm nervous. I don't know why, but I am."

"You needn't be," Victoria assured her. "Things couldn't be more perfect. You'll be fine."

"I'll keep telling myself that."

"Believe it. I better get going before Mrs. Doyle gets mad at me. I love you," she said and turned to leave.

"Well, dear," Mrs. Doyle began as she hobbled up to Jordan. "I've never seen a couple more suited for each other. I'm glad you two finally came to your senses and realized that you belong together. I've been waiting a long time for this day."

"I know. I'm sorry we kept you waiting for so long."

"May the gracious God hold you both in the palm of His hands," she said, taking Jordan's hands in hers. "And, today, may the Spirit of Love find a dwelling place in your hearts forever."

Jordan leaned into Mrs. Doyle and kissed her on the cheek. "Thank you."

"Shall we go, dear? A handsome, young man who is anxious to marry you is waiting for you downstairs."

"Yes." She nodded. "Let's go."

They walked down to the narthex, and Mrs. Doyle gave Jordan a quick squeeze before heading to her seat.

The music started, and, one by one, the bridesmaids and

groomsmen proceeded toward the altar.

After the last bridesmaid and groomsman took their place and the church quieted, she drew a breath, looked up at her uncle, and smiled. He took her arm and wrapped it through his. "Are you ready?" he whispered.

She nodded.

When she stepped into the nave, the wedding march filled the silence, the guests rose from the pews, and all eyes turned toward her. She looked past the sea of people for Reed. When she saw him standing in front of the altar, the nervousness melted like wax over a flame.

Yᴏᴜ ᴍᴀʏ ᴀʟsᴏ ᴇɴᴊᴏʏ ᴛʜᴇ ғᴏʟʟᴏᴡɪɴɢ ғʀᴏᴍ ᴇXᴛᴀsʏ Bᴏᴏᴋs Iɴᴄ:

Royal Mission
Josephine Valent
December 17, 2021

What began as an evening fit for a princess ended with two men dead.

While visiting Washington, DC, Princess Dominique's life is shattered when her beloved bodyguard is murdered during an attempt to kidnap her. She can't fathom what anyone would want with her, but whatever the reason, it is apparently worth killing for.

Ethan Moore, an ex-Green Beret, knows he can't refuse to accompany her back home when the request comes from the White House. Neither Ethan nor Dominique is happy with the arrangement and, though they just met, neither is exactly dazzled by the other. He thinks she's stubborn and spoiled, and she finds him rude and arrogant. To make matters worse, the raging attraction between them seems to add fuel to the fire.

Given Ethan's impressive military record and Dominique's escape from her would-be kidnappers, his superiors believe she is no longer in danger, but it isn't long before he and Dominique discover that she is not as safe as the White House believes her to be.

When her abductors track them down, Ethan and Dominique have to find a way to get along and deal with a past scandal in order to keep their wits about them and stay one step ahead of the kidnappers. Otherwise, she could be gone forever.

EXCERPT

"Wasn't that a splendid concert, Jean Pierre?" Princess Dominique brushed aside a tress of hair that had fallen loose from her French twist. "An absolutely divine conclusion to my visit here, wouldn't you agree?" As she glanced over, she noticed Jean Pierre, ever-vigilant, scanning the Grand Foyer of the Kennedy Center. She hoped he'd been able to enjoy the performance despite the distraction of his duties.

"*Oui*," he replied. She knew when he gave a quick, inconspicuous pull on the collar of his shirt that he was focused on something. He was always on high alert. She wished he could relax enough to enjoy the perks that his employment offered.

"Jean Pierre, how many times must I remind you?" she chided as she tugged his arm. "We are in the United States and at its capital no less. We should speak English while we are here."

"*Oui*—I mean, yes. Of course." His eyes narrowed and he frowned. She followed his line of sight as he spied the hulking figure just outside on the River Terrace take a long, slow drag from a cigarette before dropping it to the ground and crushing it beneath his heel. She took note of the man's lack of grooming and wrinkled tux and assumed Jean Pierre's reaction was to his lack of polish. Jean Pierre was always impeccably dressed when he accompanied her to such events, and she knew him well enough to know it was just as much a desire to blend in as it was pride.

"It was a beautiful weekend here. It is too bad my schedule did not permit a longer stay."

"*Oui*—yes."

"Are you all right?" she asked, a slight line forming between her brows.

"Let's just say that I'd feel a little bit more comfortable if there were two of me here right now," he answered. She noticed his focus shift as he glanced down the Hall of States and his attention settled on someone maneuvering through the crowd in their direction.

"Don't be ridiculous." She gave his arm a reassuring pat. "I'm sure the president's guards have had this entire forum secured for days."

"I'm sure the president's security was the first to leave the concert, along with the president and the first lady." She felt his hand slide over her arm as he guided her back toward the Eisenhower Theater.

"Jean Pierre, why are we going back to the theater?"

"Wait for my command, Princess." He had switched back to French, and she couldn't mistake the harsh yet controlled urgency to his voice. She didn't hesitate when he quickened their pace.

"You are to pass the entrance to the theater and go through the parking exit. Then find a way out," he instructed. "Do not go back to the hotel. Go to the police. I will come and get you there."

"What is it?" she whispered, returning to French. A numbing chill raced up her spine, but she knew enough not to react.

"No longer a coincidence," he muttered.

"What about you? Will you be safe?"

"Don't worry about me, Princess."

In the same split-second the clammy fingers of a sweaty

hand clamped down on her shoulder, she heard Jean Pierre's quick, tortured scream as his hand slid from her arm and he fell to the ground. A torrent of fear whipped through her, fast and fierce.

"Keep walking, lady," the throaty voice of her assailant ordered from behind her, his thick, vile breath heavy and disgusting on her neck. "And don't make a scene or I might be forced to start shooting."

About the Author

Josephine Valent has lived and worked for most of her life in Southern California at the beach, in the city, in the country, and most recently, in the desert, which she now calls home. She enjoys taking cross-country road trips and has traveled coast to coast several times.

An avid reader growing up, she considers it liberating to open a book, leave life behind, and step into someone else's world.

When she's not immersed in the lives of the heroines she's conjuring up for her next romance novels, she's watching true crime shows.

She loves romance, dares to dream, and writes as if anything is possible and she is limited only by her imagination.

www.ingramcontent.com/pod-product-compliance
Lightning Source LLC
Chambersburg PA
CBHW061515050726
47593CB00002B/582